Prodigies: Our Greatest Hero

By

Alex R. Castro

ISBN: **0692537872**

ISBN 13: **978-0692-537879**

Prologue

Monsters Do Exist

Children often hear stories of all kinds of monsters. They read or are told stories about vampires, dragons, werewolves, and so many others. The truth is that the kinds of monsters that kids are told about don't exist. But there are monsters in the world. The monsters I am talking about are men: men who kill, rape, and destroy all over the world. This is a story about the actions of a particular group of monsters, a group of monsters that created my family.

These monsters are a terrorist group that calls itself the "Dawn of the Shadow." This group has been around for hundreds of years. It has caused death and destruction to people everywhere. Governments all over the world have fought this terrorist organization for many years. The Dawn of the Shadow has a lot of money. Its membership is in the thousands and includes ex-military personnel, politicians, businessmen, scientists, and others from all walks of life. All follow an evil ideology that advocates a new world order, and those who oppose them must be destroyed. The leadership of the Dawn of the Shadow consists of eleven individuals. No one, not even their members, knows their identity. They are known as the High Masters. Every so often, a member of the Dawn of the Shadow's lower ranks will rise and be allowed to become one of the High Masters. For someone to rise to this position of leadership, he must engage in some action that advances the cause of the terrorist group significantly.

One individual who is on the verge of being admitted to the High Masters is Nicholas Hammerstein. At six feet tall, he is a well-built man with black-and-grayish hair. His brilliance is matched only by his ruthless evil. He has killed countless people over the years in service of the Dawn of the Shadow. In intelligence circles he is known as the "Creator," because he successfully masterminds horrific acts of international terrorism. What the High Masters appreciate about Hammerstein is his visionary thinking and ambition. Killing, for him, is not something that he does just to advance the cause of the Dawn of the Shadow; it's something he enjoys. Nicholas Hammerstein is himself a brilliant scientist in the field of genetics.

His right-hand man is Paul Bisping, a man known in intelligence circles as "Ajax," after the ancient Greek warrior. Ajax is a former special forces operative from the British Army. He is as tough as nails. He is a bald warrior who stands six feet two and is extremely muscular, with tattoos of skeletons across his chest and back. Like Hammerstein, Ajax likes not only to kill his victims but also to make them suffer.

Hammerstein has convinced the High Masters to support a plot that will assure the terrorist organization's victory over the rest of the world. The High Masters will then run the world. As a member of the High Masters, Nicholas Hammerstein would be one of those rulers. This plot is known in the intelligence community as the "Prodigy Project."

Hammerstein and Ajax have convinced the High Masters that the genetically modified eggs that Hammerstein has created, when combined with the semen from the right male candidates, will produce prodigies. Hammerstein extracted the knowledge of how to create these eggs by kidnapping and torturing the world's greatest genetic scientists. Once Hammerstein got the knowledge he needed from them, those scientists were disposed of. Although the eggs were artificial and modified, due to the nature of the process the semen had to be natural, from a live male specimen. This meant that Hammerstein and Ajax had to kidnap and forcibly remove the semen from a male victim. Once the natural semen was combined with the modified eggs, a prodigy would be born. At least, that was what Hammerstein believed. If the semen were compatible with the modified eggs, the prodigies created would be individuals with superhuman powers. Once those powers were under the control of the Dawn of the Shadow, the world would be theirs to control. After all, no human army could stand against an army of prodigies.

Hammerstein, Ajax, and fifty trained military soldiers committed to the Dawn of the Shadow's cause traveled the world to find candidates for the Prodigy Project. Together they kidnapped and tortured young healthy men all over the world. They took the semen from these men by force and combined the semen with the modified eggs. If the prodigy children were created, then those men were allowed to live for further experimentation. If not, then the kidnapped men were disposed of. This usually meant a bullet to the head.

Over the course of years, Hammerstein and Ajax kidnapped, tortured, and killed hundreds of young men in the prime of their lives. Although Ajax enjoyed the suffering they inflicted, the High Masters were not pleased with the persistent failure of the Prodigy Project. The High Masters financed and supplied everything Hammerstein needed for success. But not a single prodigy was created. The High Masters communicated to Hammerstein that time was running out, not only for his Prodigy Project, but for Hammerstein to become one of the High Masters.

With the knowledge that the High Masters' patience was running thin, Hammerstein decided to target US military personnel for the Prodigy Project. Hammerstein felt he would kill two birds with one stone. If he could not succeed with the Prodigy Project, then he would at least be killing as many of the US military as possible. Either way, it worked to the advantage of the Dawn of the Shadow.

The type of individual that Hammerstein needed for his Prodigy Project was one who was in perfect health. Someone who had no disease, someone physically fit, someone who did not drink or smoke. At the same time, it had to be someone the world would not necessarily miss. Then Hammerstein had an "a-ha" moment: there are no better candidates than the best warriors in the United States—Navy SEALs.

Chapter 1

The Trap

The US government had been in constant battle with the Dawn of the Shadow. American intelligence was always listening for any chatter related to the secret group's activities. One day the CIA got intelligence that the Dawn of the Shadow was going to have a gathering of the High Masters at a location in Syria. The entire US government, including the president, felt that it would be a major blow to the Dawn of the Shadow if any of the High Masters were either captured or killed. This was intel that could not be ignored.

Orders were given to dispatch a team of Navy SEALs to the location. This was SEAL Team 3. Their mission was to capture or kill any Dawn of the Shadow leaders that they could find. The team consisted of fifteen tough, seasoned soldiers. One of the SEALs was named Jordan Reyes, an African American man with no family. He was committed to serving his country. He was a man who always believed in doing what was right. This man would become my father.

The intel that was given to the SEALs was that the High Masters would be meeting at a heavily guarded private house in Syria. The house belonged to a member of the Syrian upper-class elite, Mahmoud Iqbal. Mahmoud

Iqbal was part of the Bashar al-Assad regime. He was well known to be anti-West. Therefore, intelligence officials felt it likely that Iqbal could be part of Dawn of the Shadow.

The SEALs landed in Syria in the stealth of night, by parachute. They quickly assembled and mobilized on their targeted location: a huge mansion on about ten acres of land. They counted thirty guards. Back in Washington DC, the president and his staff watched a camera feed supplied by an aerial drone. One by one the SEALs took out all the guards by sniper fire or by strangulation from behind. The SEALs quickly made their way into the mansion. As they got deeper and deeper into the mansion, they saw no signs of life. Outside, four SEALs remained to stand guard.

Suddenly, drones that were monitoring the action on the ground were blown out of the sky. Washington lost all visual contact with the mission and the SEALs. The SEALs that were guarding the premises came under heavy fire from all sides. They were caught off guard. It seemed as if whoever was firing upon them had come out of nowhere.

The SEALs in the mansion rushed out to help their comrades. They had walked into a trap. Reyes and the SEALs lost contact with their men outside the mansion. They also lost contact with their sniper. In the distance and on the roofs of the mansion dark figures fired upon them. They tried to take defensive measures and fought back valiantly. However, the SEALs noticed that their bullets were just bouncing off their attackers.

Reyes and the other SEALs saw that their attackers had red eyes. These dark figures with red eyes seemed like demons to Reyes.

Finally, one of his comrades was struck and fell to the ground. Reyes ran to help him. To Reyes's surprise, he found no blood and no bullet wound. There was, however, a dart-like weapon in the man's neck. Reyes realized at that moment that the enemy was trying to capture—not kill—him and his men. More SEALs fell as the dart-like projectiles rained upon them.

Reyes was the last one standing. One dart entered him and then another. Reyes felt his limbs becoming numb and he began to lose consciousness. But he would not give up. The shadowy figures got closer and closer. Reyes aimed his weapon at them, but the drugs that were in the dark projectiles kept him from firing.

He fell to the ground and managed to turn onto his back. If he could just pull the pin on a grenade, he could at least blow up some of the assailants with him. As the shadowy figures got closer, Reyes reached for a grenade. But as he did so, a boot came down on his hand, stopping him from getting it. Reyes looked up.

It was Ajax. Reyes recognized him from the military briefing that was given before this mission. Ajax, smiling, looked down on Reyes and said, "Not so fast, dog. We need you alive." Then Ajax took the butt of his

M-16 weapon and smashed it down on Reyes's head. That blow, along with the drugs, knocked Reyes unconscious.

***

The Pentagon was in shock. They had lost all communication with the SEALs and deployed more drones to the area. However, once the drones came to the area where the SEALs were attacked, there was nothing to see. The video relayed over satellite showed only an empty and deserted mansion. There were no members of SEAL Team 3 anywhere, nor was there any sign of their attackers—not even the guards that the SEALs had killed.

It was clear to the generals at the Pentagon that this had been a trap from the start. It was also clear that whoever did this was aware of SEAL tactics and the gaurds that the SEALs killed were sacrificed for the enemy's real targets. Eventually, The United States military got more military personnel on the ground, but there was still no sign of any of the SEALs. It was as if they had just vanished. The president did not want this military failure known, so he announced that the SEALs had been shot down in a helicopter. The generals at the Pentagon, the secretary of state, and the president all had the same burning questions: Why did they want to capture the SEALs? Was it for the enemy to gather intel? Was it to publicly behead them as a strike against the West?

No one had any answers. However, they all had the same fear: wherever the SEALs were, they were as good as dead or worse.

Chapter 2

From Torture Comes Life

Reyes and the rest of his SEAL team woke up many hours later. When they did, they found themselves naked and chained to a wall about ten feet from one another. Their arms were outstretched to their sides and their feet were chained to the wall in a crucifix-type position. My dad, Reyes, was chained last out of his team of fifteen. They had been stripped of their uniforms and weaponry while rendered unconscious by the drug in the dart-like projectiles.

The SEALs noticed that they were in a large warehouse. They were hurt, muscles sore, limbs chained, and mouths gagged. Despite these conditions, their first instinct upon awakening was to find a way out and look for any weaknesses from the enemy. Unfortunately, they could find none. There were armed men all around them. There were ten on a level above them and fifteen on the main floor where the SEALs were. My father and the other SEALs figured that there had to be more men outside.

The warehouse was huge. It was about half the size of a football field. In the middle of the ground floor were three large capsules. They appeared to be the type of capsules or containers that people are placed in when they are healing from an injury, or to exercise damaged muscles. The capsules were about four feet high and two feet wide. The capsules had what appeared to be water in them. Next to the capsules was a table with all different kinds of unknown chemicals.

It was my father's guess that he and his platoon would be tortured. The enemy was going to try to get whatever information they could about the US military operation. At least, that was what my dad and the other captured SEALs believed.

After about fifteen minutes, more men came into the area. One of the men was the same man who had smashed my dad in the face—the one known as Ajax. All the SEALs recognized him from military briefings. Orders were always to kill Ajax on sight. He was responsible for killing a lot of people over the years, including many Americans.

In his thick British accent, Ajax yelled to the other men present in the warehouse, "Hey, fellas, it appears all our guests are awake, eh. Let us give them a proper greeting, shall we?"

The armed men began to laugh. Ajax took off his shirt. He had muscles on top of muscles. Ajax then gave a loud speech to the SEALs about where they were being held.

He said, "You Navy SEALs are probably wondering where you are. I have good news. You're back home in

America. In fact, you're in Durham, North Carolina. You see, you are Navy SEALs. You are SEAL Team 3. You just disappeared in Syria, so the entire US government has been looking for you. But they are looking for you all over the world, in places like the Middle East, Europe, and Asia. They are not looking for you here in the United States. That is why we smuggled you back here—because this is the last place they will look for you. This way, the boss can conduct his little experiments on you in peace for as long as he wants, eh."

Ajax went up to the first of the Navy SEALs chained to the wall. This was the one on the very opposite end from where my father was. Ajax said, "But first it's time for me to have my morning workout, eh." He laughed. The other armed men again began to laugh as well. They knew what was about to happen.

Ajax began to throw punches viciously and repeatedly at the first Navy SEAL. Blows to the head. Blows to the body. Ajax's punches were fast and hard. Blood began flowing from the chained SEAL. Ajax stopped before the SEAL lost consciousness.

Then he began on the next SEAL and repeated the process of throwing punches. Each SEAL received dozens of blows. Each SEAL that was next to the SEAL currently being beaten braced himself mentally for his turn. Finally, Ajax, sweaty from all the punches he had thrown, got to the last SEAL, my father.

Ajax looked at my dad and said, "Hello, hello, hello. Save the best for last, eh." Then, as he had done to the other fourteen SEALs, Ajax began beating my father mercilessly. Blow after blow, my father knew he could not take much more of this.

Finally, a commanding voice in the background yelled, "Enough!"

Ajax looked at my father, disappointed he could not beat him some more.

Each SEAL was battered and bloody. However, they were all curious who had commanded Ajax to stop. They were about to find out. The individual, wearing a black military uniform, walked to the table in the middle of the warehouse floor. He had a commanding presence. Everyone felt it. Every one of the armed men and Ajax stood at attention to what he was going to say. This unfamiliar figure scanned all the SEALs with a determined look.

Then in a clear, articulate, commanding voice, he said to the SEALs, "Greetings, gentlemen. I am Nicholas Hammerstein, commonly known in the intelligence community as the 'Creator.'" Indeed, he was known in the intelligence community as well as throughout special forces units in the US military. Hammerstein continued, "You obviously fell for our trap in Syria. The intel that was supplied to your CIA was supplied by me. The Dawn of the Shadow has people all over the world. We even have people inside your military machine. Getting the United States to send its best was easy.

Cutting all communications between you and Washington was easy. Removing all satellite and drone footage was easy. It was easy thanks to the help of our people who are inside your government. Now you are wondering—I'm sure—why you are all still alive."

My father and his unit were indeed wondering that.

The madman then said, "No, it's not to extract intel from you with endless torture. It's to allow you to participate in a project that will change the world. The project that I am referring to is the Prodigy Project."

Even in their weakened and beaten state, my father and his fellow SEALs were shocked by what they had heard. They had heard of the Prodigy Project but never believed it was true; it sounded like misinformation, spread to hide what the Creator was really up to.

Hammerstein—the Creator—said, "You are the best the military has to offer. You are all prepared to die for your country. Well, be prepared to die now for the cause of the Dawn of the Shadow." He laughed, and the sinister sound sent a chill down the spines of these hardened SEALs, including my father.

Then the Creator took out a big, twelve-inch blade. He walked up to the first SEAL out of the fifteen, a twenty-nine-year-old who only wanted to serve his country. The SEAL's name was John Hicks. Hicks squirmed in his chains to try to somehow get away from Hammerstein, but it was hopeless. The chains were too strong.

Hammerstein had two of his men walk up to Hicks. One held several twenty-inch tubes. The other held a two-pint container that had one end of a tube attached to it. The fourteen other SEALs, including my father, feared what was going to happen to Hicks.

Hammerstein then took the knife and cut into Hicks. Hicks, still with the gag over his mouth, let out a muffled scream. My father and the other SEALs felt anger and frustration that they were chained and could not help their suffering comrade. After Hammerstein cut into Hicks, the man holding the tubes inserted one into Hicks. Blood was dripping on the floor. From the tube came a white substance. The white substance flowed into the container held by the other armed henchman. Once the container was halfway filled, the tube was removed from Hicks, and the container had a small cap placed upon it. A third of Hammerstein's men came and quickly blocked the wound so that Hicks would not bleed to death. It was painful for my dad and his fellow SEALs to watch. However, for the members of the Dawn of the Shadow, it was pure entertainment.

Hammerstein made sure that he had gloves on. He even put on a white coat. Then, with glee, Hammerstein took the contents of the capsule. He added strange chemicals and substances to the fluid that was taken out of Hicks. Hammerstein worked at an enthusiastic and gleeful pace. The evil madman was like a person who knew that he had a winning lottery ticket. It was just a matter of scratching away the substance hiding the number. This adding and mixing of substances took close to fifteen minutes. Finally, the mixture in one of the glass containers turned green.

Hammerstein's eyes filled with rage. He then let out a scream and took out his blade and cut Hicks's throat ear to ear, killing him. Hammerstein looked at Hicks's dead body and yelled, "You were worthless to me!" Then he turned to the SEAL next to Hicks and said, "You're next."

One by one, over the course of the next several hours, Hammerstein repeated the process that he had started with Hicks. He would forcibly take fluid out of his captive, put it in a sterilized container, and then mix it with strange substances and chemicals. Then the mysterious mixture would turn green. The madman, in his rage at seeing the color, would kill the SEAL whose fluid he had just extracted.

My father was horrified. His comrades didn't deserve to die on a wall like this. My father's emotion went from fear to rage until finally he had to accept what was happening. He saw no way of escaping. He knew in his heart that it was only a matter of time before his throat would be cut like his comrades'. After my father's comrades were murdered in front of his eyes, their bodies were just left there hanging from the wall. My father wished that his captors would at least cut them down and bury their bodies.

Hammerstein remained focused on what he was doing. Soon he was down to the last four SEALs: Evans, Rubin, Mathews, and, the last on the wall, my father.

Hammerstein paused his unholy procedure and became engrossed in his chemicals.

My father and his remaining comrades, still gagged and chained, had no idea what Hammerstein was doing. They just wanted this torture to be over. They wished that Hammerstein or one of his men would just end their suffering with a bullet to the head.

After thirty tense minutes of Hammerstein working with the chemicals on his table, he turned to face the remaining SEALs. An excited look was in his eye. Hammerstein then did to Evans, Rubin, and Mathews what he had done to the other SEALs. He stabbed them one after another and collected the fluid from all three at the same time.

Hammerstein then looked at my father and said in a sinister tone, "Don't worry, dog. I have not forgotten about you. Your turn will come."

Hammerstein then took fluid from each SEAL and again combined it with the strange substance and the chemicals on his table. He mixed the chemicals as he did before, taking special care to keep the containers separate. This time the substance did not turn green. Instead, it turned blue.

Hammerstein let out an unholy laugh and yelled, "Success!" He then took the containers holding the blue substance and put them in the large, water-filled capsule. He commanded his men to quickly set up the recording devices, and they configured four very sophisticated cameras. These cameras would record everything that took place in the warehouse.

Ajax then came to Hammerstein and said, "Sir, it's almost time for you to give your presentation to the High Masters."

Hammerstein responded in an annoyed manner, saying, "Yes, yes, I know. We have to have this completed before I give the presentation." He commanded one of his men to inject the capsules with the growth-accelerating solution. The man poured a small capsule of clear substance into each tube.

My father and the other SEALs were amazed at what they saw. It was clear that in each capsule was a life form. Each looked like a small embryo at first but then grew larger and larger. Finally, to my father's horror, what he saw in the capsules looked to be three humanoid figures. He thought to himself, *Is this what the Prodigy Project is? Some form of cloning?* My father was about to find out it was so much more.

Hammerstein looked at the tubes and said, "Grow, my little prodigies, grow!" In the capsules, the three figures grew into babies. Hammerstein and his men carefully took the small babies, one by one, out of the capsules, making sure to handle them with the utmost care. The babies were not moving. Oxygen masks were placed on their faces. Then Hammerstein's men cleaned the chemicals from their little bodies and put them into three separate plastic containers.

Hammerstein and his men waited. The babies showed no signs of life; no movement in their chests showed that they were breathing.

After five tense minutes, Hammerstein let out a scream of pure rage. "This is a failure, a failure!" He took out a gun and ran up to Evans, Rubin, and Mathews and shot each one in the head, execution style. Then he yelled a horrific order to his men: "Take those damn pieces of trash and discard them in the garbage where they belong." Hammerstein was talking about the motionless babies on the table. Apparently his experiment had not worked. The babies had not survived. One of his men took out three garbage bags and opened them. Then Ajax picked up each baby, discarded each in a separate bag, and tied it shut. Then the bags were thrown into a Dumpster outside the warehouse. My father was amazed at how heartless Hammerstein was. He felt that even though those children had been created through some evil experimentation for some evil purpose, they were still children and did not deserve to be thrown away like garbage.

Hammerstein was running out of time. Soon the High Masters would want his "presentation," and he had no prodigies to show them. Hammerstein was down to one SEAL: my father. Hammerstein walked up to him and grabbed my father by the throat with his left hand and took out his twelve-inch blade with his right hand. He held the blade up to my father's eyes and said with incredible anger, "You better pray that your semen works, and my prodigies are created. You see, I am really angry right now. You're the last hope I have of this project working. If this project does not work with you, I am going to take this knife and cut you to pieces while you're alive. After all, a man has to do something as a way of relieving stress." Then Hammerstein said sarcastically, "I am sure you understand."

Hammerstein then turned to his men and yelled, "Clean the capsules and the table and prepare to repeat the process." His men quickly emptied out the capsules that had contained the three babies. A new supply of the strange substances and chemicals were added to the table. Hammerstein then went up to my father with his cleaned and sterilized twelve-inch blade. There his two men stood ready to collect the substance from my father's body. Hammerstein stabbed my father in an area above his groin. My father felt an intense, sharp pain from the blade. Like the SEALs before him, he let out a scream even though he had a gag in his mouth. The tubes were placed inside my father, and the white substance came out. Then one of the men took a hot metal rod and cauterized my father's wound. The semen was mixed with the other substances and chemicals. My father hoped that the color would be green. This way they'd just kill him; his misery would end, and Hammerstein's mysterious plot would fail.

After the mixing took place, a color began to form. Hammerstein and my father waited with bated breath. One hoping for blue, the other praying for green. After three minutes the chemicals began to form a color. Hammerstein gasped at what he saw. The color was *blue*. In a small container was not one life form, but three. The three life forms were my two brothers and I. This is how we were created.

Hammerstein yelled at his men with excitement, "Quickly, open the capsules and ready the growth-accelerating formula." Hammerstein gently picked up a small substance and placed it inside the first capsule. He did this two more times for the other two capsules. One of his men poured a clear substance into each capsule like before. Then Hammerstein placed my brothers and I in three separate capsules. Again everyone watched in awe as the three life forms started to grow. Like before, they grew into three babies. Three male babies. Each looked as if he weighed about eight pounds. Hammerstein gently removed each one from its capsule, wiped away any chemical residue, and dried it off. Like the first three babies, these babies were motionless. No signs of life or breathing. Hammerstein frantically affixed small oxygen masks to their faces. Then he placed the infants in plastic sterilized containers. Hammerstein looked intensely at the motionless babies in the containers. He seemed almost like a father concerned about his sick children.

With a very intense and even desperate voice, Hammerstein yelled, "Breathe, my little prodigies, breathe!" Then after twenty tense seconds passed, the chests of the three babies started to go up and down. They were *breathing*. They were alive and breathing like any newborn baby. However, they were not awake. They were asleep. This was due to an invisible gas that acted as a sedative, which they inhaled along with the oxygen that Hammerstein gave them. This was to Hammerstein's delight. He could not contain his incredible joy. He laughed and yelled, "Yes! I did it. I did it. Success, success!"

My father put his head down in despair.

Chapter 3

The Presentation

Hammerstein had a huge smile on his face that just would not come off. He went up to my father and said, "Congratulations, SEAL. You have helped me make history." Hammerstein pointed at my sleeping brothers and me and loudly said, "Those children, my children, will change the world." He walked away from my father victoriously and then gave a command, "Prepare...for...the...presentation."

Ajax looked at Hammerstein and said, "Five minutes, sir."

Hammerstein looked at Ajax and nodded confidently.

The armed men then set up three strange devices about thirty feet apart. The devices began to make a humming sound; then a yellow glowing light shot from them ten feet into the air. This happened for all three devices as the same time. The glowing energies collided with one another and formed a huge holographic screen in the air. Hammerstein, Ajax, and all the armed men present dropped to one knee. The holograph showed eleven hooded figures against a dark background. Only their mouths could be seen clearly.

My father understood what he was seeing. More importantly, he understood *whom* he was seeing. He was seeing the original targets for his mission. He was looking upon the High Masters, the leaders of the Dawn of the Shadow, the ones that even someone such as Hammerstein must answer to.

One of the hooded figures, speaking in a deep scratchy voice, said, "All may rise." Everyone stood. That same hooded figure said to Hammerstein, "You may speak."

Hammerstein looked at the screen and spoke loudly and with great enthusiasm. "Thank you, my lord. I—thanks to your support—have made history. With my creation we will end the war, and the Dawn of the Shadow will rule this world. I have created three individuals. Three...very...very...special...individuals. Individuals with powers that will allow us to crush any army and any government that stands before us. I extracted the semen from a live subject. I then combined that semen with the artificial and modified eggs that I developed. Now, after years of trial and error, I have found success, my lords."

This unholy collection of evil brought to my father's mind an attorney giving oral argument before an appellate or supreme court. In such a setting, the judges sit up high, asking questions of the attorney beneath them. In this case the High Masters were the judges, and Hammerstein was the attorney making his case. My father grudgingly had to admit that Hammerstein might be a monster, but he was truly a master orator.

One of the High Masters asked, "We can see behind you the specimens that you used to extract the semen. Your plan to trap and kidnap the Navy SEALs was a success. Now we can see all but one of the fifteen are dead. It's clear that for the first fourteen, their semen was not compatible with the modified eggs. Why? Why was only this pathetic creature's semen compatible while the others were not?"

"My lords, in order for the Prodigy Project to work, the specimen had to be in perfect health. No disease. No illness. He had to be someone who did not drink or smoke. This pathetic creature, this SEAL, was such an individual. More so than his now-dead comrades."

The High Master asked, "What will you do with him now?"

"I intend to do further tests on him. His semen works well with the chemicals. If the Prodigy Project was successful once, I believe it can be replicated. From him we can potentially spawn an army of prodigies."

The High Master responded with a curious, "Hmmm."

Then another High Master said in an impatient tone, "Tell us about what you have created so far."

Hammerstein replied enthusiastically, "Yes, my lord." Then he began the main part of his speech, talking louder and with even more excitement in his voice. "Let me introduce you to the very special beings that I have created.

"The first is a being with superhuman strength. He will be so strong that he will be able to bend and break solid steel with his bare hands. He will have the strength to crush a man's skull like a grape. No tank will be able to stop him. He will be able to lift incredible weights with ease. Also this same being will be nearly indestructible. Bullets, explosives, fire, falling from thirty thousand feet in the air will not kill him. No military ground force will be able to withstand his might.

"Next we have a being who does not have superstrength but instead superspeed. Instead of withstanding bullets, his speed will be such that he will be able to dodge bullets. No human on earth will be able to match his quickness. He will be able to kill anyone, anywhere, and no one will see him coming or going. In addition, he has a reflexive photographic memory. He can just look at any athletic movement and easily duplicate that same movement. Whether it's a gymnastics flip or a technique from the world of martial arts, he will be able to mimic that movement. He will become a martial arts master. Combine this with his speed, and no fighter on earth will be able to stand against him. He will become the world's greatest assassin.

"Last but not least, my lords, the most dangerous of the three. One who has neither superstrength nor superspeed. However, his brain has been enhanced to the point that he will be able to process information faster and more efficiently than any brain on earth. His mind will work faster than the fastest computer. He will be able to create weaponry limited only by his—or should I say our—imagination, weapons even more powerful than a nuclear weapon. His mind will advance our weapons technology so far beyond the rest of the world that no army will stand against us.

"These three remarkable individuals will work for the cause of the Dawn of the Shadow." Hammerstein yelled louder as he concluded his speech. "My lords, my gifts to you—my gifts to the world—are the greatest killers mankind has ever seen. I give to you...the prodigies!" As Hammerstein laughed, and Ajax presented the three babies—my brothers and me—for the High Masters to look at more closely.

We each still had on an oxygen mask. We were asleep, thanks to the sedative we were given. We were in separate plastic containers. Ajax pushed us out on a large cart with wheels.

The High Masters looked intensely into their holographic screen from whatever dark location in the world they occupied.

Hammerstein, Ajax, and the other men present remained quiet, waiting for a response. All they could hear from the holographic images was whispering.

Finally, after more than two minutes, one of the High Masters began to speak. "Tell me, Hammerstein, when will the powers of these...prodigies begin to manifest?"

Hammerstein responded quickly, "My lord, their powers are scheduled to manifest in about six months' time."

Another hooded figure then said, "Hammerstein, as you know, to be a killer requires more than just the ability to kill, even if that ability is extraordinary. It also requires a *willingness* to kill. While these...prodigies may have remarkable abilities that will enable them to kill and destroy with great effectiveness, what guarantee can you give that they will have the *coldness* and *ruthlessness* required to kill without hesitation and remorse? And what assurances do we have that they can and will be controlled by us?"

Hammerstein smiled and said, "Two excellent questions, my lord. You are correct. To kill requires more than just having superabilities. It requires a mind-set to act without hesitation and remorse." Ajax handed Hammerstein a silver box. Hammerstein opened the box and took out a small, glowing, silver chip. Hammerstein continued, "I will implant a chip like this in the brain of each prodigy. This will allow me to implant the memories that I see fit. These memories will enable me to condition them to be the cold-blooded killers that we need. In answering your second question, my lord, these chips will also enable me to condition their minds to the point that they submit absolutely to your will and the rest of the High Masters."

The High Master who had asked those two questions said, "Hmm." He smiled and hissed, "Excellent."

Then another High Master said something that Hammerstein had been waiting for. "Hammerstein, you have done well. You have earned a place among us. Bring the prodigies to our location. We will discuss your future in a more senior leadership role."

Hammerstein bowed his head and enthusiastically said, "Yes, my lord."

Chapter 4

The Escape

As quickly as the large holographic image of the High Masters appeared, it disappeared. The glowing energy that was in the air vanished. The three devices that the energy came from seemed to automatically turn off on their own.

Hammerstein smiled. Ajax also smiled at his superior's triumphs. Hammerstein then joyfully yelled out an order. "All right, men. Let's begin the extraction. I don't want to be in North Carolina any longer than I have to. Prepare the prodigies and the SEAL for transport. Dispose of the bodies. Leave no trace of our presence here."

With those commands, the men started to pack their gear. They had four vans. They brought three of the vans into the warehouse. They began to load their equipment into one van. They loaded the chemicals and modified eggs into another van.

My father felt that if everything Hammerstein said were true, then he had to somehow get free and escape. *But how?* Still chained, gagged, beaten, stabbed, and weakened. Surrounded by armed killers. *How?*

Then a miracle happened. My father noticed on the ground next his feet, directly beneath his hands, were chips of the wall. He looked at his wrist. He was amazed that, in his pain and suffering, he had failed to notice that his squirming against his chains had loosened the wall to which the chains were attached. He decided that he would focus on trying to break not the chains but the wall to which they were attached. So, with a quiet desperation, he slowly worked his wrist out of the wall. My father did this by twisting and turning the chain. The more he did this, the more the wall crumbled where the chains were attached.

My father had to be careful. He had to pull and twist on the chains as quietly as possible. He always made sure he looked around before he pulled. Over the course of thirty minutes, he finally was able to weaken the wall surrounding the chains. Now all he had to do was pull his arms out of the wall with the chains still on his wrist.

My father noticed each of Hammerstein's men had a sidearm, a communication device, about four grenades over their shoulders, a dagger, and an M-16. He figured that, if he could kill just one of these armed men and take his weapons, he would have a fighting chance to escape.

Every so often one of the guards would come up to my dad and taunt him. It seemed they each wanted to take a turn taunting one of the best warriors that America had to offer, a Navy SEAL. These armed men of the Dawn of the Shadow were so twisted, they even taunted the dead SEALs that were still hanging chained to the wall.

My father waited patiently. He had his head down with his eyes closed. He waited until one of the armed men got close to him. He could tell when they did by the smell. Finally one of the armed men got within six inches of my dad's face. He began to taunt my father. My father realized he had only one chance at this, and he was going to make the most of it. He took a deep breath and, with all of his might, pulled his chained arms out of the wall. He grabbed the back of the armed guard's head with his right hand and the man's chin with his left. With all his strength, my father twisted his arms clockwise, breaking the man's neck. My father acted with incredible, vicious speed and focus. With a *crack*, the armed man died instantly. My father fell forward on top of the now-dead guard. He quickly searched his body for any type of key. After a desperate pat down, he found some keys. Frantically he tried the keys on the locks attached to his leg chains. Finally he found the right key and got his legs free. Then he got the chains off his wrist. He took off the pants and boots of the armed man and put them on. Then he took all of the man's weapons.

My father went into combat mode instantaneously. He scanned the huge warehouse and saw twelve men standing guard on a catwalk fifty feet above him. Hammerstein was talking to two of his men in the middle of the warehouse. My brothers and I were in a single container right next to Hammerstein. My father did not see Ajax. There were four men at the entrance to the warehouse. Three black military vans with two men per van waited inside. This meant there might have been as many as twenty-five guys somewhere outside. My father also noticed that there were four columns in different parts of the warehouse. It looked as if the columns supported the roof. If they were as weak as the wall he had just pulled himself out of, then a few well-placed explosives would bring down the entire building.

My father would one day tell me that, at that moment, he remembered that Ajax earlier had said that they were all now in North Carolina. He thought that, if he could escape this warehouse, he had a chance of getting to safety. My father knew that he could not leave without my brothers and me. No matter what, he was not going to allow Hammerstein to use us as tools of destruction upon the world. My father was determined to escape with us. However, after taking a quick glance at the wall he had been chained to, he saw his fallen comrades. Hammerstein and his men had left them there dead just for entertainment purposes. His fellow Navy SEALs, who had been beaten and slaughtered. They were like fourteen brothers to my father. My father did not want only to escape with my brothers and me; he also wanted payback.

With determination and focus, he took the pins out of three grenades and threw them one at a time with incredible speed and accuracy at three of the four beams holding up the roof. Before the grenades exploded, he fired upon Hammerstein and the two men with him. The grenades exploded almost simultaneously with a loud *ka-boom, ka-boom, ka-boom*. My father, being a Navy SEAL, was an expert marksman. He managed to take out the two men. Two head shots. *Pow, pow!* He tried to shoot and kill Hammerstein, but, at the last minute, Hammerstein moved out of the way.

The beams made a loud *cracking* sound. They were crumbling. My father quickly threw the last grenade at the entrance where four of the guards were. With another *ka-boom* the explosion killed the four guards. Hammerstein and his men were caught completely unaware. In less than thirty seconds, my father managed to take out six of Hammerstein's men, plus the one whose neck my dad had broken. That made seven.

My father laid down enough fire at Hammerstein that he was forced to run for cover away from the babies. Hammerstein jumped behind some crates and returned fire at my dad with his sidearm. The three posts collapsed. This caused much of the roof to start to cave in on everyone. The twelve men on the catwalk all fell to the ground amid the collapsing beams. My father then took the M-16 and shot the gas tanks of two of the vans. This caused two more explosions. Between these explosions and the roof coming down, five more of Hammerstein's men were killed. With frantic speed, ignoring the soreness of his muscles from being chained to a wall, my father ran up to the plastic container holding my brothers and me and wheeled us into the back of the third van. The men on the outside would be coming in any second. Debris fell from the roof. Soon everyone and everything in the warehouse would be crushed. Then my father turned and saw Hammerstein come seemingly out of nowhere. Hammerstein leaped at my father with the same twelve-inch blade that he had stabbed him and his fourteen comrades with.

Meanwhile, Ajax and the rest of the men were trying to get inside to help Hammerstein, but the flames from the explosions and the debris stopped them. Clutching the dagger, Hammerstein's right hand plunged down on my father. Fortunately, with his left hand, my dad caught Hammerstein's wrist in the air. My father took the dagger he had removed from the first guard and swung it in a circular motion at Hammerstein's neck. But Hammerstein was tough. He caught my father's wrist and stopped his deathblow. With flames leaping around them and the warehouse collapsing, the two enemies were locked in mortal combat. Both had hate for the other in their eyes: one for torturing and killing his comrades, the other for posing a threat to his ambitions to rule the world.

Hammerstein, while straining all his muscles to drive his dagger into my father and trying to prevent my father's dagger from being plunged into him, said, "These...are...my...children."

My father responded, while straining all his muscles as well, "No...they are not."

Hammerstein was starting to win this battle of strength. His dagger was getting closer and closer to my father's throat. My father realized he was going to lose this dance of death due to his weakened condition. That's when my father decided to do an athletic move. He let his weight fall backward and used Hammerstein's momentum to make him fall forward. In a classic judo move, my father, while falling backward, placed his right foot on Hammerstein's groin. Hammerstein was surprised by the move and could not stop it. Then, with all his might and while on his back, my father made a big thrust upward with his right foot and pulled Hammerstein over him.

Hammerstein went flying through the air, helpless to stop the move. "What the...!" he screamed and then landed on his back, momentarily stunned.

My father jumped into the van with my brothers and me. Miraculously the keys were on the dashboard. My father was prepared to hotwire it but was thankful he did not have to. He started the van. He knew that he could not go out the front entrance. Ajax and his men were waiting with their guns, ready to shoot him as he came out. What Ajax and his men did not know was that my dad would not give up. He reversed the van thirty feet and spun it around so the front of the van faced the other end of the warehouse, where there was no entrance, only a wall. Debris fell from the crumbling warehouse. My father spotted more grenades in the van. He got out, took the pins out of four grenades at the same time, and threw them with all his might at the wall.

Ka-boom, ka-boom, ka-boom, ka-boom went the grenades as they exploded against the wall. The wall was damaged, but it did not come down.

My father got into the van. He had no choice but to ram the wall. He revved up the engine.

Hammerstein yelled in the background, "You can't escape with my children! They are mine. I will find you and make you suffer, no matter how long it takes, no matter...where...on...the...earth...you...go.
Do...you...hear...me?"

My father heard every word, but it did not stop him. He pressed the gas all the way to the floor. The tires screeched, and the van roared forward and smashed through the wall. At last, my father was free from the warehouse. He quickly found a road nearby and got on it.

Hammerstein came out of the warehouse in a rage, tired and dusty and coughing from the smoke from the fire. He yelled at Ajax and the other men, "Go after him! Now!" Ajax and five of the remaining twenty-five men got into the remaining van and went after my father, determined to make him suffer. The chase was on.

The warehouse was located in the Durham area. Locals had heard the explosions and gunfire and saw the flames from the warehouse. Local fire and police came to the area in the opposite direction from my father and the forces of evil. My dad noticed that we still had small oxygen masks on. We were not only breathing oxygen but some type of sleeping gas. *It made sense*, my father thought. How could hardened killers tolerate three crying babies? Even if they were prodigies. Better to keep them sleeping.

My father saw the police and the fire department coming in the distance. He also knew that Hammerstein and his men were behind him. With a two-minute head start on them, he stopped the van on the side of the road. There were trees everywhere. Grabbing my brothers and me, he cut the front seatbelts out of the van and took all the equipment he could carry, including a 9mm SIG Sauer sidearm, a twelve-inch blade, a black military-type uniform, two backpacks, and a GPS device. He ran with us, pausing at the edge of the woods to throw a grenade at the gas tank of the van. The grenade and the van exploded.

The fire department and the police stopped to investigate and put out the flames in the van. This blocked the road in both directions. Hammerstein, Ajax, and his men came to the van as well. They opened fire upon the police and fire department. The police were outmatched and outgunned. All the police and fire personnel were killed, but not before one of the police officers called a distress signal through his communication device. The Durham police now came with full force. Hammerstein and Ajax knew that they could not stay there. Ajax looked into the burning van and saw no bodies. Nor did he see the container that held my brothers and me. Hammerstein said about my father, "He must be on foot." Indeed, my father was on foot. However, Hammerstein did not know which direction my father had gone, east or west.

My father had gone east. He used the twelve-inch blade to cut up the backpacks and the belts from the van. He made a makeshift baby carrier, one that would allow him to carry two babies on his back and one on his chest. He put my brothers on his back and securely fastened them. Then he placed me on his chest and, using pieces of the backpacks, fastened me to his front. He even made sure that the makeshift baby carrier had little holes so we could put our feet through.

Now my dad was on foot. Carrying a twelve-inch dagger, a 9mm gun, the last grenade from the van, a GPS device, and three babies.

He managed to get to a subdivision. My father was starving, hurt, and tired. He looked for a house in the subdivision that had someone in a driveway, someone with an SUV. He saw a white male about five feet eight, wearing jeans and a blue T-shirt. He looked like he might have been going out to see some friends. It was dark but not late. My father went up to the man and did something that he did not want to do. Desperate and on the run, he did the only thing that he felt he could do.

He took out his firearm while carrying my brothers and me and, in a desperate voice, said, "Give me the keys to the SUV." My father had no intention of shooting the man. He felt that if the man refused, he would just hit him over the head and take the vehicle. However, the man saw the desperation in my father's eyes. He took out his keys and pressed the button to unlock the car. Then he handed the keys over to my dad. My dad took the keys and put his gun away. Before my dad got into the car, with sadness in his eyes he looked at the man and said, "I am really sorry about this. Please forgive me. One day I will pay you back."

The man said to my father something unexpected. "I believe you." The man must have felt that my father was sincere. He also must have felt that an SUV was not as important as the three babies that this desperate man was carrying.

My father said to the man, "From the bottom of my heart, thank you." Then he took us and got into the SUV. He needed to hurry up and leave, in case Hammerstein and his men were close. He started the car and was about to drive off.

But before he did, the other man said, "Wait." The man reached into his pocket and pulled out his wallet. From the wallet he took out two hundred dollars. With his hand outstretched, he said, "Take this. You are going to need money to feed those babies. Not to mention a bunch of diapers."

My father, in awe, asked, "What is your name?"

The man said, "Barry Samson."

My father said, "One day I am going to pay you back. Good-bye." Then my father drove off, realizing that even though there was evil in the world, there was also good.

As he drove, many thoughts raced through his mind. He was at last in a place where he did not have to worry about Hammerstein and his men. He was able to think more broadly about what was going on.

Despite all that had happened, my father felt grateful. He was grateful that he had escaped with us. He was grateful that he now had the SUV, a little money in his pocket, and some weaponry. But he was most grateful that he had stopped Hammerstein's plan to turn my brothers and me into killers.

My father thought long and hard as to what Hammerstein said to the High Masters. Over and over again, he asked himself the same question. *Do these children really have superpowers? How could it be possible?* He also remembered Hammerstein saying to the High Masters that their powers would manifest in six months.

Where could I go? he thought. *Who could I trust with these children?* Hammerstein had said that the Dawn of the Shadow had people inside the US government. That was how he and the rest of his SEAL team were set up and trapped in Syria.

People with superpowers can't be real. My father was a simple soldier; he could not believe that the babies in his possession had superpowers. *Can they?* But although he did not believe in beings with superpowers, he could not deny what he'd just experienced. He also could not deny that even though Hammerstein was evil, he might not be a liar. And despite his hate for Hammerstein, he had to acknowledge that the man was brilliant.

Why would someone so brilliant go through all the trouble to create these children, unless what Hammerstein had told the High Masters were true? My father had no answers to his own questions.

He then made a firm decision. Whether or not these babies had powers, they were special, and they had to be kept out of Hammerstein's possession at all cost. If they did have special abilities, he could not risk them being used as some type of superhuman weapon against the world. *I will raise them*, he thought to himself. Raise them to be prodigies of good, not evil. Prodigies of helping people, not hurting people.

My father felt something else as well. He felt a connection to us. He felt...love. Yes, it's true a madman in a warehouse had created us for some sinister purpose. However, we were not just any kids. He had felt it ever since watching us growing in the capsule: We were his children. Though we had been created by evil, we had come from him, and we were innocent. We were *his sons*.

Like any good father, he was going to do whatever he could to take care of his children. *Hammerstein would have raised us with hate*. My father was determined to raise us with love. He would go back to where he had been born and raised: Brooklyn, New York. He would remain hidden there and somehow he would raise my brothers and me.

Chapter 5

Being on the Run

Sadly, the SUV was not the last thing my father would steal. He now had three mouths to feed. While traveling on the road from North Carolina to New York, my father had to steal again and again. He robbed several convenience stores for cash, always at gunpoint. Every time my father robbed someone, he always apologized and said he would pay the person back one day. He meant it. My father was a good man. As good as they come. However, he was desperate. He knew an international terrorist organization was after him. He also knew he could not risk his sons falling into the hands of the US government. He was on his own. He could not even take money out of his own bank account because he had no identification. So, he stole. He stole baby diapers, baby food, baby car seats, baby clothes. He even stole baby toys.

My brothers and I no longer had the sedative in our systems that Hammerstein used to keep us asleep. We were awake and filled with life like any other babies. We cried and cried and cried. We stayed up through much of the night. Even for this tough Navy SEAL, it was difficult dealing with three babies on his own.

My father would pull off the road to feed us and change our diapers. He sang to us, held us, and rocked us to sleep, many times holding two of us at the same time. He struggled with the fact that, if he got one of us asleep, the other two would cry and wake the one he'd just put to sleep. It was hard, really hard. My father felt far more comfortable in a firefight with evil terrorist than he did taking on three babies. The good news was, he was a trained Navy SEAL. A big part of the Navy SEAL training is going long periods of time without sleep. Sometimes more than twenty-four hours. He needed that training now that he had three newborn babies on his hands. It was hard, but my father was a true warrior. He never gave up. He never stopped trying to do his best to take care of us. Despite the challenges, his love for us only grew. This love made him even more determined to be the best father he could be.

One day he decided to give us names. This helped him keep track of us, since we all looked alike. He named my brothers Joshua and Jahvon. He named me Jason.

After traveling on the road north for over fourteen hours, my father finally got to New York City. He had about five hundred dollars in his pocket. So he decided to go to a motel to stay. My father knew that he could not continue to steal to provide for us. He had to somehow get a job. Something that could provide what he desperately needed to raise his boys: stability.

At a local Internet lounge, he searched online for jobs. He looked at the help wanted section of every newspaper he could find. But his searches led to nothing.

He needed something that would allow him to work and at the same time be close to us. He could not have a typical nine-to-five job that required him to be away all day. He did not want to risk leaving us with a babysitter. He needed a work-from-home job of some kind. But he was not able to find anything. He needed help, and he wished to speak to one friend in particular, but he was afraid to. The Dawn of the Shadow had intel on all of SEAL Team 3. The probably also had intel on the team's families. Now his entire unit was dead; only he was alive. My father did not have family himself, but he did have friends. And he was not going to take any chances with their lives. He was on his own.

***

My father had to continue to spend money to feed himself and us, plus pay for a motel. He was once again down to having only two hundred dollars. Again his desperation grew. Finally, on the third day of being in the motel, my father read an ad in the newspaper that gave him hope. It was an ad to work in a restaurant kitchen. It was an Italian restaurant called Ferrante's, named after the owner, Salvatore Ferrante. It was not a prestigious job by any means, just sweeping, mopping floors, and taking out garbage.

My father managed to get a pair of jeans, some shoes, and a shirt with a collar. He cleaned himself up as best he could. He also had stolen, on his road trip from North

Carolina, a three-baby stroller. He pushed my brothers and me to the local train. He then took the train to the neighborhood the restaurant was in. It was in a prestigious part of Brooklyn—Brooklyn Heights.

My father found the address of the location. He walked into the front entrance. He made sure that my brothers and I had bottles of milk to keep us occupied as he went for his job interview. The restaurant was pretty big. It was about 10:30 a.m. on a Thursday morning during September.

A lady at the front desk greeted my father, smiling. "Good morning, may I help you?"

My father responded, "I am here to see about the position of kitchen worker." The lady seemed a bit surprised. As if she'd never seen a man apply for a job with three babies with him. She invited my dad to sit at one of the booths while she got the owner. My father waited for about five minutes. It was his instinct as a soldier to always be ready for action. Even while he was going for a job interview. Then my father noticed a five-foot-seven-inch, somewhat chubby man walk toward him. He had on glasses, and his black hair was balding. He looked to be in his midfifties. The man approached my dad, and my dad got up from the booth and the two men shook hands. The man was Salvatore Ferrante himself, the owner.

He said to my dad in a strong Italian accent, "So you want to work here in the kitchen?"

My father responded immediately, "Yes, sir, I do."

Mr. Ferrante asked my father some very basic questions. "Can you sweep?"

"Yes, sir."

"Can you mop?"

"Yes, sir."

"Can you take out garbage?"

"Yes, sir."

"Then you're hired," Mr. Ferrante said with a big smile. He laughed, and he and my father again shook hands.

"Thank you, sir."

Mr. Ferrante noticed the three babies. "These are all your sons?"

"Yes, they are."

Mr. Ferrante looked troubled and said, "You know I don't pay enough for you to support three children in an expensive city like New York. I only pay ten dollars an hour."

My father's response was understanding and a little bit nervous because now the real negotiations had begun. My father took a deep breath and said, "Mr. Ferrante, I noticed an ad in the paper for an apartment for rent above this restaurant."

Mr. Ferrante said, "Yes, of course. I own the building. I have tenants on every floor. I have a room for rent on the second level right above the kitchen. The rent I am charging is three thousand dollars a month. This includes utilities. It's a one-bedroom. You would not be able to afford that if you are only making sixteen hundred dollars a month at ten dollars an hour."

My father anticipated that response. He said, "Mr. Ferrante, sir. I am a father of three, as you can see. What is most important to me is that my boys have a place to stay. Not the money. I propose that you allow me and my boys to live upstairs. Just pay me two hundred dollars a month. That will be enough for me to buy baby food and diapers for the kids. You won't have to pay a dime more. This is a restaurant. So I know all the food does not get eaten. I will eat from what is left over. With your permission, of course."

Mr. Ferrante looked down at my brothers and me. We all smiled at him when he looked at us and made funny baby noises at him. He smiled back. Mr. Ferrante was a good man. He was also a man who had a strong love for children. After all, he had five children himself. Mr. Ferrante looked into my father's eyes and saw him for what he was at that moment: a desperate man.

After forty seconds of very tense silence, Mr. Ferrante said, "All right, you got it."

My father felt once again the same way he had felt in North Carolina, when Barry Samson gave him the SUV and the $200. That there were good people in the world. People worth fighting for. Then my father made a silent prayer, thanking God for today's blessing and for sending this angel in the form of Mr. Ferrante.

Mr. Ferrante took my father upstairs to the second level, where we would all be living. He led my father through the back of the restaurant into the kitchen. Mr. Ferrante introduced my father to everyone. My father wheeled us through the kitchen and out the back. The back led to the other side of the building and the stairs to the second level. My father carried the three of us in the stroller up the stairs, following Mr. Ferrante. There were two doors for the two apartments on this floor. Mr. Ferrante let my father into the one closest to the stairs. My father was very pleased. It was a decent, one-bedroom apartment with a hardwood floor. There was a television, refrigerator, couch, and a hardwood table in the kitchen. My dad asked about his neighbor who lived down the hall.

Mr. Ferrante, in an annoyed tone, said, "I don't like him. I can't wait for his lease to be up in the next year. That's Bobby. He is not really a friendly guy. He is one of those really liberal guys who has a strong love for animals. He has animals in his room. Even a real big snake. I told Bobby that I better not see any of the animals out of his room."

My father said, "OK, thanks for telling me about him and his snake."

My father then took us back to the motel and got the rest of his stuff, including his weapons, and came back to settle in our new home.

Chapter 6

The Price of Failure

While my father was trying to find a stable living situation for all of us, Hammerstein had the burden of facing the High Masters. Hammerstein had to explain his failure: how he'd allowed my father to escape with my brothers and me. Hammerstein and his right hand, Ajax, were truly dangerous men. They feared no one on earth, with one major exception. They feared the High Masters, the rulers of the Dawn of the Shadow. The High Masters despised failure. The penalty for failure often was death. Hammerstein and Ajax knew they could not hide. So they decided to face the High Masters directly and take whatever punishment awaited them.

Days after my father's escape, Hammerstein, Ajax, and the remaining twenty-five of the fifty men that were originally part of Hammerstein's team went to one of the locations where the High Masters gathered.

This particular location was in Paris, France. Hammerstein and his team gathered in one of the churches in Paris, a front for the Dawn of the Shadow.

Nervously the men walked into the church. Here they would face the High Masters in person. They all walked through a room in the back of the church. The room had a passageway through the wall. The passageway led to a cave-like tunnel with torches to light the way. They continued down for about two hundred feet. Deep underground, the passageway opened onto a very sophisticated area guarded by armed men. Hammerstein and his men were very familiar with this location. They knew exactly where to go. They walked toward the back of the location. As they did, a man appeared in front of Hammerstein. It was a man whose face had been disfigured. He was six feet tall with an athletic build and wore a sidearm. Hammerstein and the man were very familiar with each other. They were rivals. Though the two men were members of the Dawn of the Shadow, they hated each other. Both men had ambitions to become a High Master. The disfigured man's real name was not known in the intel community. He was known as the Extractor.

The Extractor walked up to Hammerstein. The other men paused for the unfriendly encounter between the two rivals.

"Welcome back to Paris, Creator," the Extractor said.

Hammerstein said nothing but looked at him intensely.

The Extractor spoke in an amused manner. "I see this Prodigy Project of yours has met with failure. Defeated by a mere grunt." The Extractor looked at Ajax and smiled with disfigured lips. "Not even your pet Ajax here was able to stop the grunt from stealing your precious prodigies."

Ajax snarled and stepped forward to confront the Extractor.

Hammerstein put a hand on Ajax's chest to hold him back. He then looked at the Extractor and said, "Shouldn't you be in Africa with the rest of the animals?"

The Extractor smiled and said, "Yes, I will be going back there. I just wanted to see your face before you faced the High Masters." He laughed.

Hammerstein stepped closer to the Extractor, until their faces were only six inches apart. "I know you enjoy seeing me down, you dog. But at least my failures didn't leave me with a burned face. The Prodigy Project is not the only plan I have of rising to become a High Master. And once I become a High Master, one of the first things I will do is get rid of a certain disfigured undesirable within the Dawn of the Shadow."

Ajax smiled at his master, standing up to his rival.

The Extractor said nothing for ten seconds. Then he stepped aside for Hammerstein and his men. He pointed at a pair of ten-foot-high doors and said, "The High Masters await."

Hammerstein and his men proceeded to the doors, and guards opened them.

The room was huge and dark, too dark to see the ceiling.

Suddenly the eleven High Masters appeared from the shadows upon a fifteen-foot-high platform. Hammerstein, Ajax, and the rest of the men dropped to one knee.

A High Master with an American accent issued a command: "Rise."

No one said a word. Hammerstein and his men waited nervously for what was coming next. For ten seconds there was a very uncomfortable silence in this huge, dark room.

Then another High Master commanded in a powerful voice with an Arabic accent, "Creator, Ajax, do not move from the spot where you are standing if you want to live." This instruction was not given to the other twenty-five men. Suddenly ten pairs of red eyes appeared behind the High Masters. Hammerstein and Ajax did not move. The other twenty-five men took out their weapons. They would not help them. The beings with the red eyes revealed themselves. They looked like men dressed as ninjas. However, they were not human. They were sophisticated robots that moved with great agility and strength and could shape their arms into weapons, such as blades or firearms. They were the High Masters' personal guard, known as the "Blade of the Shadow."

They jumped over the High Masters. Once on the ground, they began killing Hammerstein's men. The men tried to defend themselves. They fired their weapons but to no avail; the bullets bounced off the killer robots. Some of the men were beheaded by robots whose arms had turned to blades. Others were shot dead. One robot fired out metallic tentacles that wrapped around a man's neck, pulling his head off.

One of the men figured that, if he was going to die, then he might as well die taking some High Masters with him. He pointed his pistol at the High Masters and fired, only to see a glowing field of energy surround them. The bullets bounced off the energy field. Other men tried to escape the room, only to find that the door was locked.

Hammerstein and Ajax stood motionless and watched the carnage. The screams of their dying comrades echoed through the chamber. Blood fell upon their faces.

After less than sixty seconds, the slaughter was over. The robots known as the Blade of the Shadow stepped back into the shadows of the room until only their glowing red eyes could be seen. Then the red eyes vanished.

A High Master with an Australian accent began to speak. He directed his comments at Hammerstein. "As you and Ajax are fully aware, the Dawn of the Shadow does not tolerate failure. You and Ajax have been spared due to all the positive things that the two of you have accomplished for the Dawn of the Shadow.

However, you will not always be spared if your failures continue."

Hammerstein took a deep breath as sweat poured down his forehead. "Understood...my lords."

Then a High Master with a French accent spoke. "You will no longer pursue the Prodigy Project. This American soldier is now on the loose somewhere with the prodigies. So long as the prodigies are alive and not in our control, they will pose a threat to Dawn of the Shadow."

Hammerstein interjected nervously, "They will be found, my lord. Also, with your permission, I wish to pursue my other strategy that will work in the favor of the Dawn of the Shadow."

A High Master with a Spanish accent asked, "Are you speaking of the young Ramesh Patel? It will take you ten to fifteen years to bring the plan regarding him to full fruition. Will it not?"

Hammerstein said, "Yes, my lord."

"You may pursue it. One of the strengths of the Dawn of the Shadow and the reason why we have survived for centuries is our patience in seeing our plans through," said another High Master with an American accent.

Hammerstein and Ajax were then allowed to leave the chamber, determined to find my father and make him pay for the humiliation that they suffered this day.

Chapter 7

Fatherhood

Meanwhile, back in America, the Pentagon and the CIA were trying to piece together what had happened to SEAL Team 3. The bodies of the team were found in the rubble at the warehouse in Durham, North Carolina. The bodies of all the SEALs except my father. They could see that the men had been tortured and then killed. Government officials did not know what to make of my father's absence. Was he still in the hands of the Dawn of the Shadow? Was he a traitor? They listed my father as a prisoner of war. They kept what really happened to the SEAL Team 3 classified. The demise of the fourteen other SEAL team members was reported to the media as death by a tragic helicopter crash in Syria. No one considered the possibility that the Dawn of the Shadow had insiders in the government.

As time went by, our father settled into being a guy who worked in a kitchen. This was not exactly how he had envisioned serving his country when he became a Navy SEAL, but he did his job. The days turned to weeks, the weeks turned to months. My dad was very disciplined. He had a schedule, and he stuck to it. He liked that the kitchen was close to the stairs. That way he could run up and down to check on us and make sure we were OK. He hated the idea of leaving us alone for any time. But he had no choice if he was going to work. Sometimes he would sweep, mop, and take out the garbage with one of us strapped to his back. As babies, we enjoyed the constant motion of riding on our father's back. Soon the other restaurant staff fell in love with us. My dad used the little money he had to buy us baby food and diapers. He would eat from the restaurant leftovers. He did not mind. After all, Ferrante's had the best Italian food he had ever tasted.

My father was not a big fan of his neighbor down the hall. He felt it was irresponsible to keep animals that were meant to be in the wild in an apartment.

One day my father ran into his neighbor. He asked him what kind of animals he had in his apartment. My father was especially curious about the kind of snake he had. He wanted to know how secure this snake was because he was concerned for the safety of his children. The neighbor was not a friendly man, and he scoffed at my dad.

"Mind your own business!" the neighbor yelled.

My father did not push the issue.

When he was not working, my dad would spend a lot of time holding two of us at the same time. Rocking us to sleep. He would even sing to us. His favorite song was "You Are So Beautiful" by Joe Cocker. Dad worked hard for Mr. Ferrante. He cleaned, and he cleaned well. Part of his military training was being disciplined and keeping his quarters spotless. This helped him to do a great job for Mr. Ferrante. My father believed that you should always do a job to the best of your ability. Even if it's a menial job.

Sometimes my father woke up at night from nightmares—nightmares of the torture he experienced at the hands of our creator, Hammerstein. He thought back about things that Hammerstein had said while my father was his prisoner. He remembered Hammerstein talking about our powers manifesting in six months. It had now been over eight months since my father had escaped with us. But he'd seen no changes in my brothers and me. My father began to think, *What if Hammerstein was wrong? What if Hammerstein caused so much death and suffering for nothing?* Maybe the whole notion of kids with superpowers was just some crazy idea from an evil madman. That was when my father started to look forward to a life raising three normal children.

Every day my dad played and talked with us. He liked to extend his pinkie, place it in our palms, and shake our little hands. It was our daily routine. He would make funny faces and toss us in the air. We loved it. He had dolls he played with for our entertainment. Dad loved being a soldier, but he found out that he loved being a father so much more. Over time he managed to make wooden baby cribs for each of us. Before he made the cribs, my brothers and I slept on the bed with him. He put the mattress on the floor, just to make sure we did not get injured by accidently falling off the bed at night. Now, with the cribs, Dad would be able to have the bed to himself. Also, he thought it would be safer for us.

***

One Saturday afternoon our father was off work. He was playing with us as he normally did. Then something powerful happened that would change everything. My father wanted to go downstairs to the restaurant kitchen to get some pasta to cook that night. He made sure we were all secure in our cribs, even though the cribs were low to the ground. Before my dad left, my brothers and I all held our hands out. We either wanted him to pick us up or let us grab his pinkie. We loved grabbing and shaking his pinkie. Dad was not going disappoint us. He first shook my hand with his left pinkie. Then he shook Joshua's hand with his pinkie. *Then it happened.* As my father finished shaking Joshua's hand, our genes changed within us. The genes that would give us our powers became active. It was a quick and seamless process, one that my father did not even notice. He was about to get a painful realization that our powers were now active within us, and he would have to take his parenting skills to new levels.

After Joshua let go of Dad's pinkie, it was Jahvon's turn. Jahvon stretched out his hands, flailing his arms with a big smile on his face, making happy baby sounds. Jahvon was excited to shake my dad's pinkie just like Joshua and I were.

Dad said to Jahvon, "OK, OK, OK, I'm coming, I'm coming." Then Dad smiled at Jahvon, stretched out his left pinkie, and said, "Here's your pinkie handshake, son." Jahvon reached up from his back and grabbed Daddy's pinkie, and they did the pinkie handshake. Then when my father tried to gently pull his finger away from Jahvon, my father noticed something strange. For some reason he could not pull his pinkie out of Jahvon's grip. His pinkie was stuck in the grip of nine-month-old. My father then started to feel pain. Jahvon's grip was getting tighter. Suddenly, in his excitement, Jahvon closed his grip. There was a *crack*, and my father grunted in pain. This nine-month-old baby had just broken the finger of a Navy SEAL. My father, in shock and pain, finally managed to wrestle his finger from Jahvon.

He touched his pinkie and felt sharp pain. "God dammit!" The finger was shattered.

Then a small voice said, "God dammit. God dammit. God dammit." My father quickly turned around, thinking that there was someone in the apartment with him. He got into a fighting position, ready to fight anyone who would try to take his kids from him. Even with a broken finger. But my father soon discovered there was no one in the apartment but us. Still, he kept hearing that small voice say, "God dammit."

Dad followed the sound to its source and was shocked when he found it coming from my crib. The voice was mine. Even though I was only nine months old, I was able to repeat what I heard. Then my father remembered what Hammerstein had said about our abilities. One of us would have superstrength. Another one us would have a highly developed mind. And another would have superspeed. It was clear to my father who had what ability. Jahvon had the superstrength. Dad had a broken finger as proof. My speech showed that I had the developed mind. That left Joshua as the one with superspeed.

Joshua was enjoying the show, when suddenly his body seemed to start convulsing. It was as if he were having a seizure. Then, in an explosive display of athletic ability, Joshua crawled over the gate of his crib and landed on his knees and his hands.

Dad reached out to Joshua to make sure he was OK. But as Dad approached him, Joshua, with a smile and a laugh, quickly crawled away. Joshua thought Dad was playing a game of tag with him. My father was stunned at how quickly Joshua moved for a nine-month-old.

My father sprinted and leaped after him. However, Joshua was faster. He crawled out the apartment door that my father had left open and speeded toward the head of the stairs. My father was scared that Joshua would fall down the steps and get seriously injured. Once again, with all his speed, Dad tried to reach out and snatch Joshua. My father was fast, but his nine-month-old son was faster. Joshua started down the stairs. My dad got there too late but was in awe at what he saw. Instead of seeing a baby tumble down the flight of stairs and suffer serious injury, he saw this nine-month-old display sufficient depth perception, agility, and speed to acrobatically cartwheel down the stairs without getting hurt. Still ignoring the pain of his broken pinkie, my father ran down the stairs. Joshua took off out the open back door. My father got outside, and what he discovered terrified him. He saw a smiling and laughing Joshua facing him, ready to continue the game of tag. However, Joshua's back was to the street. My father feared that if Joshua crawled out into the street, he would be run over by oncoming traffic. Dad made no sudden moves. He just bent down on one knee and outstretched his arms, as if to invite Joshua to hug him. However, Joshua was not moving; he wanted Daddy to chase after him again. My father did not know what to do.

Meanwhile, back upstairs in the apartment, Jahvon and I were alone. Jahvon saw Dad chase Joshua out of the apartment. In his baby's mind, Jahvon wanted to participate in the game too. With one big downward swing of his baby arms, Jahvon smashed the bars of the wooden crib. He was now free to go find and "play" with Daddy and Joshua. Jahvon crawled toward the apartment door. Every time his hands hit the ground, they made a loud *boom,* as if an adult were stomping his foot. The workers in the kitchen below thought that my dad was working out upstairs with dumbbells and dropping them on the floor.

When Jahvon got out of the apartment and into the hallway, he saw the stairs and started toward them. But a sound distracted him. A loud hissing and rattling sound. It came from behind Jahvon, from the neighbor's apartment. Still on all fours, he did a 180-degree turn and saw a slithering figure by the neighbor's front door.

It was the snake that my father had been worried about. It was not just any snake; it was the highly poisonous diamondback rattlesnake. These snakes have venom that can kill a human. The diamondback was about five feet in length and had beautiful diamond-shaped markings on its body. These snakes make the rattle sound as a way of warning other creatures to stay away from them, or they will strike. Unfortunately, Jahvon, being just a baby, was highly attracted to the rattle sound of the snake. The sound of it just drew him closer. Crawling on his hands and knees, he charged down the hall toward the snake. Jahvon had a big smile on his face and was even laughing. As far as this nine-month-old was concerned, he had found himself a toy to play with.

As Jahvon got within two feet of the dangerous animal, the snake with blinding speed struck out at him. Its fangs closed on Jahvon's shoulder. However, the snake was unable to penetrate Jahvon's skin. Jahvon was a prodigy. He had superstrength and was created to survive bullets and bombs. A snakebite, even one from an animal as dangerous as the diamondback, meant nothing to a superhuman, even one only nine-months-old. The sharp fangs of the diamondback broke in half on Jahvon's steel-like skin. Jahvon then grabbed the snake's throat with his left hand and its tail with his right. The snake thrashed about, trying to escape. For this snake, however, there was no escape. For Jahvon, on the other hand, he had himself a new toy to play with.

Back outside, unaware what Jahvon was doing with the snake, my father was still trying to figure out how to get to Joshua without causing him to crawl into the street and get hit by a car. Then a miracle happened. In the trees above the sidewalk a bird chirped. Joshua, being a baby curious about life, looked up when he heard the sound. He wanted to know what it was. My father saw Joshua distracted and took advantage of the moment. With all his might and speed, he took two big steps and leaped with his body outstretched as far it could go. He managed to grab Joshua by the legs.

"Gotcha!" Daddy yelled out.

Joshua began to cry. His game of tag had just come to an end.

With Joshua securely in his arms, my father went back to check on Jahvon and me. When he got upstairs, he was horrified by what he saw.

Jahvon's little body had the slithering coils of a five-foot killer around him. My father put Joshua in our apartment and closed the door behind him. Dad took out his handgun, determined to kill the animal. At the same time he thought of the horror of having to pull the lifeless body of his son away from this snake. As my father closed in on the snake to shoot it, he was shocked by what he saw. The snake did not have his nine-month-old baby boy. Rather, it was his nine-month-old baby boy who had the snake. Jahvon had a huge smile on his face. He was laughing, having the time of his life with his new toy.

My father, his gun still pointed at the snake, put his other hand out to grab the snake's head. He knew that was where the snake was most dangerous because of the fangs. Just as he had earlier with his pinkie, my dad had to wrestle the neck of the snake away from the steel grip of his son. After about fifteen seconds of trying, he finally did it. My father put his gun away and used his two hands to securely hold the snake. He opened the snake's mouth and saw that its fangs had been broken in half.

My father noticed that Bobby's apartment door was open. He called out Bobby's name. Bobby did not answer. My dad looked at the snake and said, "You're lucky my son was nicer than Hercules." Then he threw the snake with all his might into Bobby's apartment and closed the door.

Jahvon began crying. Just like Joshua, Jahvon's fun had abruptly ended.

My father went to pick up his son from the floor to take him back to the apartment. As he did, he let out a groan. Picking up this nine-month-old baby felt like picking up a solid steel thirty-five-pound dumbbell. This was due to Jahvon's increased density and hard skin.

My father got us all in the apartment. He closed the doors and windows so Joshua could not get out.

Later he told Mr. Ferrante about the snake escaping Bobby's apartment. It was determined that Bobby had left the apartment without properly locking either his door or the snake's cage. Mr. Ferrante apologized to my father and started the eviction procedure against Bobby to get him out for being negligent in watching that dangerous snake.

My father had a burning thought as he bandaged his broken pinkie: *It was all true. Everything that monster Hammerstein said was true.* His three sons, whom he loved dearly, truly had superpowers. By keeping them hidden, he had made the right decision. He could not raise three superhuman kids—who were being hunted by the world's most dangerous terrorist organization—the same way most fathers would raise their sons. He had to take special precautions.

Each of us had different needs that my father had to be careful of. For example, to make sure Joshua did not crawl away when Dad took us for walks, he now fastened a leash around the trunk of Joshua's body. To make sure that our superstrong brother did not accidently hurt either me or Joshua, Dad built Jahvon a steel crib, one that he could not break out of.

For me, well, Dad had to make sure that he did not curse or swear. I was worse than a parrot. Everything he said, I said right back to him. He learned the hard way that he even had to be careful with what I heard from television.

One day Dad had the TV on, and one character said to another, "Screw you, lady."

Later, when my dad took us shopping, a lady looked down at my brothers and me in our stroller, smiled, and said, "Aw, look how cute you boys are."

My response was a loud, "Screw you, lady." Dad quickly wheeled us away and out of the store.

My father started to take notes on our powers. He realized that Joshua had a huge appetite. Daddy had to feed him five times as much as he needed to feed Jahvon and me. Joshua was much like a cheetah. He burned energy rapidly due to his quick movements and needed to consume a lot of calories. I was like a computer. I was talking when I was one year old. I had a photographic memory. Everything I heard and read, I easily remembered.

***

As the years went by and we got older, we became more and more comfortable with our powers. We continued to live in the apartment and stayed in the shadow of the world. By the time I was two years old, I was fluent in twenty languages. I was already a whiz at math. My father put me on the Internet, and I absorbed everything I saw. I was a true genius. I could read an entire four-hundred-page book in three minutes and remember every sentence.

We decided that we would make our birthday the same date as our father's, May 15. This way we could all celebrate our birthdays together. We all loved one another. My brothers and I worshipped our dad. He was everything to us. Even though he had no powers himself, we hung on to his every word and nearly always obeyed him without question. Sometimes there were disagreements, though. For example, Jahvon was a huge sports fan. Football was his favorite. But my father would not let Jahvon join a football league. He could not risk Jahvon accidently killing another kid with a tackle.

We all felt a certain sadness that came from the isolation. Our powers kept us from being among other kids.

My father used my high intellect to his advantage. He made me my brothers' teacher and had me homeschool them in the apartment. My father even got me a blackboard to use. Dad understood the importance and the value of education. Having superpowers did not exempt us from getting an education. I taught my brothers math, science, social studies, English, and Spanish. They did not like having to do homework assigned by their brother, but those were Dad's orders. For my father there was another benefit of homeschooling my brothers: it allowed us all to stay out of the public eye. My father knew that if he tried to put us in a school, there would be too much exposure and too many questions. He kept us as hidden as possible.

Chapter 8

Time in the Kitchen

When we got older, my brothers and I would sometimes visit our dad at work. It had been eight years since my father escaped from Hammerstein and got a job in the kitchen. Mr. Ferrante became like an uncle to us. We loved him, and he loved us as well. The bond between Mr. Ferrante and my dad became very strong over the years.

One day, while I was in the kitchen, I tasted the pasta sauce made by Mr. Ferrante's chefs. When I tasted it, I acknowledged that it was good, but I decided to experiment by making some modifications to the ingredients.

A few days later when my dad, Mr. Ferrante, and other chefs were all in the kitchen, I politely asked Mr. Ferrante to try my pasta sauce. Mr. Ferrante was amused. He had working for him some of the best chefs from Italy. It was not possible that some African American kid could make pasta sauce better than what he was used to, but he was willing to indulge me just to be kind. So he did me the honor of tasting it. I put some of the sauce in a spoon and held the spoon up to his mouth with my right hand. I had my left hand under the spoon just to make sure none of the sauce spilled on the ground.

Mr. Ferrante tasted the sauce. "Hmm, let me taste it again," he said. So I gave him some more. "Wow, I don't believe it," he said. "This is the best pasta sauce I have ever tasted, Jason." Then he asked, "How did you make it?"

Feeling really proud, I told him about the modifications I made with the ingredients.

My father was pleasantly surprised to see Mr. Ferrante so happy with my sauce.

Mr. Ferrante insisted on using the sauce I made in his restaurant. His chefs felt insulted at first. They wondered, who was this kid that the boss would favor his sauce over theirs? After they tasted the sauce, they wondered no more. They were blown away by my creation. Everyone was.

Soon Mr. Ferrante's business increased, all because of the sauce I made. It went great with all the pasta. Mr. Ferrante started generating more and more revenue. About eight months after I created my pasta sauce, Mr. Ferrante opened another restaurant in Manhattan. He was so grateful to my family and me that he increased my father's wages. Mr. Ferrante even put together a plan to sell my sauce in the supermarkets, and he offered my father a partnership. Mr. Ferrante wanted to give my family and me credit for helping his business become even more successful. However, my father said no. He told Mr. Ferrante that he could keep all the credit for the sauce and all the revenue.

My father would not tell Mr. Ferrante that we still had to remain as hidden as possible. I did not mind. I understood that my father's first priority was to protect us. At this time our first line of defense was staying as hidden as possible. Hammerstein and the Dawn of the Shadow were still out there. Mr. Ferrante still insisted on showing his gratitude in any way he could. He moved us into a three-bedroom apartment in his building. He got us flat-screen TVs, new clothes, and all the food we could eat. This really helped my dad with Joshua's appetite. Mr. Ferrante always made sure my father had more than enough money in his pocket to take care of us. He even let my father drive one of his cars anytime he wanted. Meanwhile, Mr. Ferrante was making hundreds of thousands of dollars in revenue from the grocery-store sales and the increased traffic in his restaurants. As far as Mr. Ferrante was concerned, he was not doing enough for us.

Chapter 9

Lessons about Life

My father thought about what I had done with the pasta sauce. This was an example of how our abilities could bring something positive to the world. In this case, a very tasty pasta sauce. This was my father's dream for us. To do things and create things to benefit society. To help people. That was his vision for us. Not be to tools of death and destruction.

My father taught us lessons about life whenever he could. One lesson I never forgot was when he invited my brothers and me to come to the window of our apartment. The window faced a very busy street called Baltic Avenue. From our window we could see the corner of the block where people were constantly crossing. There was always a lot of traffic.

Dad said to us, "Look at that lady in the green shirt with the cell phone." We watched the lady talking on her cell phone, walking to the corner. She had started crossing the street without checking to see if the light was red to stop oncoming traffic. By the time she got about five feet into the street, a driver beeped his horn at her. She jumped, startled. She was so concerned about her conversation on her phone that she was not even aware that the light had changed. Over the course of fifteen minutes, my father pointed out other men and women who all did the same thing. People who were not at all aware of what was going on around them.

My father said to us in a very firm voice, "Sons, always be aware of your surroundings. Is that clear?"

My brothers and I simultaneously said, "Yes, Daddy."

My father responded approvingly, "Good." Then he gave us all a kiss on the forehead.

My father took us for walks about the city. He always hid his face anytime he went someplace where there were a lot of cameras. He did not want to risk showing up on a camera networked to the technology of the Dawn of the Shadow. That would make it easier for the Dawn of the Shadow to find him and us.

As time went by, my brothers and I did what we could to help people. My father allowed Jahvon and Joshua to patrol on their own for a limited period of time during the day. He had them wear hoodies to keep their faces covered. One time a lady was pushing a baby in a stroller across the street. The light was red and the lady with the stroller had the right of way to cross. A taxi driver was speeding out of control because his brakes were not working. The taxi was about to collide with the lady and her baby when Jahvon leaped up in the air about twenty feet and landed between the lady pushing the stroller and the out-of-control taxi. The lady closed her eyes, fearing she and her baby were as good as dead. However, the taxi smashed into Jahvon. Jahvon, with his superstrength, blocked the taxi. When it hit him, the front of the taxi caved in. The airbag opened up, protecting the driver from injury. Jahvon was not moved at all by the three-ton vehicle traveling at fifty miles per hour. He leaped away before anyone could see his face.

Another time a lady had her purse stolen by a thief. The thief moved like a bolt of lightning. Suddenly something tripped him from behind, and the thief fell to the ground. The purse vanished from his hand. It was Joshua. He returned the purse to its owner and ran off. Because of the speed at which he moved—too fast for the lady to see his face—she must have felt some type of ghost had helped her.

We would help society whenever and wherever we could. We made sure to be as discreet and inconspicuous as possible when we used our powers. Our goal was to help without attracting attention. We were successful at it.

It made us feel good when we helped people. Helping people made my brothers and me so happy, we wanted to do it all the time. Just like comic book superheroes.

We enjoyed reading comic books. We read about comic characters and their abilities, and we said to ourselves, "We can outdo these superheroes."

Jahvon would say things like, "That superhero is strong, but I bet I'm stronger."

My brothers and I were very playful. We got into arguments sometimes, but we loved one another very much. We each had our own style, too. Jahvon loved to have a big afro. He felt he was like Samson from the story in the Bible. Maybe he believed subconsciously that his superstrength had something to do with his hair. Joshua and I, for the most part, kept a very low Caesar-style haircut. That was the same kind of haircut my father had. Sometimes Joshua would go with the Mohawk haircut. My dad was very willing to allow us to express ourselves in terms of style and look. However, he made one thing very clear: no tattoos.

Daddy never told us the whole story as to how or why we were different from other kids. He never even explained why we did not have a mother. He always would say, "You boys are not ready to hear about the past. When you are ready, I will tell you everything."

When we turned eleven years old, my father decided to take us somewhere where we could be alone. He wanted to take us out of the city, at least temporarily. Some place where he could properly train us and develop our powers. My father knew it was only a matter of time before my brothers and I would face evil. This thought saddened him. It also filled him with fear. He knew that no matter our powers, a resourceful evil organization like the Dawn of the Shadow had the potential to destroy us.

Dad had asked Mr. Ferrante for permission to take a couple of weeks off. He also asked Mr. Ferrante if he could take my brothers and me to the cabin that Mr. Ferrante had up in the Pocono Mountains in Pennsylvania.

Mr. Ferrante said, "Sure, no problem."

So one Friday morning we packed our clothes and a lot of food. This included a lot of pasta. We all loved pasta, especially Joshua. We made sure to pack food for eight people. Twenty-five percent of the food we packed was for me, Jahvon, and Dad. The other 75 percent was for Joshua alone. That's how much of an appetite he had. It was amazing because he had this skinny body, but he was muscular. He had the physique of a young amateur boxer. Jahvon was thick and stocky. He had the body of a young fullback. I was just skinny. Both of my brothers were about an inch taller than me. I felt jealous of my brothers because I was the smallest and the weakest.

Chapter 10

Training in the Poconos

We made the trip to the Pocono Mountains in Pennsylvania. It was our first road trip. At least, it was the first one that we remembered. We drove for over two hours, listening to music, reading comics, and watching a movie as Daddy drove. We enjoyed the ride. We used the GPS in the SUV to find Mr. Ferrante's house in the mountains. It was a house that Mr. Ferrante did not go to that often. It was a nice wooden house in the middle of a wooded area in Stroudsburg, Pennsylvania. The next closest house was about a mile away. This suited my dad fine. He wanted us to be as alone as possible.

My dad had brought his weapons, the same ones he had taken from the Dawn of the Shadow and maintained over the years. On the way to the Poconos, he stopped in a small town and bought even more weapons at a gun store: two machine guns, a shotgun, a rifle, and hundreds of rounds of ammunition. My brothers and I wondered why Daddy was getting so many guns. It seemed as if he were getting ready for a war. This was a very progun area, and the store did not even check for identification. They just wanted the money. Thanks to Mr. Ferrante's appreciation for his new pasta sauce, my dad had a lot of cash on him.

We all got settled into the cabin. It was pretty big, and we each had our own room. However, there was no electricity. We had to keep warm by the fireplace. There was no TV. That was disappointing to us. My brothers and I all had our favorite shows. Especially on Cartoon Network. We were diehard *Justice League* fans.

After we got unpacked, we went out and played some catch with the football. We were amazed when deer ran by. We even saw a black bear roaming in the distance. Here nature was a really big part of living. Not like in the city.

After playing catch and looking at the area, Daddy had my brothers and me prepare dinner. I was the best cook in the family, but Daddy felt my brothers should share some of the burden as well. After we ate our pasta and fruits, Daddy told us our true purpose for coming up here in the mountains. It was not to just enjoy the sights and nature. Tomorrow we would begin training.

"There is evil in this world," he said in a somber tone. "One day you are going to have to face it. When that day comes, I want you to be ready. Now go get some rest."

He gave us all a kiss and a hug. Then we got our sleeping bags ready.

The following day after breakfast, Daddy took us on a long walk. I noticed that he had his firearm with him. I never liked guns. We walked to where there was a huge cliff. The view was incredible; we could see so much vegetation from where we were. The sky was such a beautiful blue. There was a breeze, but it was very comfortable even though it was fall. Not too hot and not too cold. We walked to the top of a huge cliff. Daddy asked us if we could see the bottom of the cliff. We all tried. We were really high up. It was scary. We were so high that we could not see the bottom.

Dad then smiled and said, "I'm willing to bet that we are about ten stories up from the bottom. I am also willing to bet that at the bottom are probably rocks." As Daddy was talking, I noticed that he slowly walked behind Jahvon. I did not understand why. He continued: "I believe that if anyone were to fall from here, they would face a certain death." Suddenly he took his right foot, put it on Jahvon's butt, and, with all his might, pushed Jahvon over the edge of the cliff. Joshua and I were horrified as we heard Jahvon's scream, and he fell to what we believed was certain death.

We all heard from the bottom a loud *boom*. Joshua and I pleaded with our father as to why he had just killed our brother.

Daddy smiled and said, "Just listen."

Miraculously we heard Jahvon's voice from the bottom of the cliff. It echoed from the surrounding cliffs. "Hey, I...I am OK."

Daddy responded by laughing and yelling down, "Of course you're OK, son. After all, you're practically indestructible. Did you really think a fall like this would hurt or even kill you? I could throw you out of a plane at thirty thousand feet, and you would still be OK."

Joshua and I and especially Jahvon were all dumbfounded. Daddy knew that Jahvon would be able to survive even though he had fallen over ten stories onto rocks.

That kick in the butt was the start of training.

Jahvon yelled in a bit of a frustrated tone, "Daddy, how am I going to get back up?"

Daddy smiled. "Jump, son, jump. Jump as high as you can. If you can't jump all the way up, then use your strength and stick your fingers into the side of the cliff walls and climb up."

Jahvon's voice was filled with self-doubt. "OK, Daddy." He bent his knees and jumped as high as he could. But he was able to jump only thirty feet high, and then he fell back down, making a loud *boom* sound. The ground shook where he landed.

He had to jump much higher than thirty feet to get back to us. So he jumped again, and this time used his strength to stick his fingers into the rock. Then he began to climb up and up and up. Climbers must always climb with the fear that one mistake could cost them their life. Not for Jahvon. Jahvon had a smile on his face because he knew that if he fell, he would be OK. And fall he did. After trying a couple of times over the course of twenty minutes—climbing and then slipping and falling and trying again—he finally made it to the top. When he got back we all had a smile.

Jahvon felt so proud of himself, he yelled: "Yahoo! Watch out, bad guys, I am indestructible. Yahoo!" His victorious cry echoed throughout the whole area.

Dad gave Jahvon a kiss on the forehead and said, "Well done, son. I am proud of you."

Jahvon, all excited, said, "Daddy, Daddy, can I jump down there again? Huh? Huh? Please, Daddy."

Daddy said, "You got it, son. Go for it." With that permission, Jahvon took two steps back and jumped up in the air as high as he could.

Jahvon yelled with joy, "Yahoo!" He fell back down the ten-story-high cliff, crashing down with a *boom* again. Then he repeated the process of using his strength to climb back up.

After letting Jahvon show off for about an hour, Daddy laughed and said, "OK, son, that's enough. It's time to move on."

Jahvon said, "OK, that was fun."

***

It was clear that Dad was going to find different ways to see our powers and how they worked, and, most importantly, to get my brothers comfortable with their abilities. This training was really designed more for my brothers. I was a supergenius. However, my biggest weakness was my lack of confidence. As the days went by, he gave my brothers different tasks, and he gave us all lectures about our powers.

One day he took out the guns that he had taken from the Dawn of the Shadow. He told Joshua and me to get behind him. Then he had Jahvon take off his shirt and go back fifteen feet. He aimed a gun directly at Jahvon's chest. Joshua and I and especially Jahvon were really nervous about Daddy pointing a gun at Jahvon. However, we trusted our daddy.

My father began firing his weapon at Jahvon. The gun was loaded with hollow-point bullets, but they bounced right off Jahvon's chest and head. None of the bullets hurt him. After it was clear that the bullets would not hurt him, Daddy stopped shooting. He did not want to waste all of his ammunition. Jahvon again was enjoying the moment.

Daddy then had Jahvon pick up the SUV. The SUV was a Ford truck. It weighed about three tons. Jahvon lifted it with ease. Daddy instructed him to press the truck over his head until he could not do it anymore. Jahvon was able to do it about ten times before he got tired. I did a math calculation and determined that his max lift was about fifteen tons. Not bad for a twelve-year-old. Then

Daddy had Jahvon jump as high as he could from a standing position. He had him jump as far as he could from a standing from position. Then Daddy had Jahvon jump for height and distance with a running start. Over and over again, he recorded what Jahvon was doing. Jahvon could jump as high as fifty feet with a running start. He could jump forty feet standing flat-footed. With a running start, he could leap a distance of about one hundred feet.

One day after Daddy finished training with Jahvon, the two of them went to collect wood for the fireplace while Joshua and I made dinner. As Daddy and Jahvon gathered the split logs that daddy had cut earlier, Jahvon started to boast. Jahvon felt really proud of himself and his superpowers. Perhaps too proud.

"Daddy, I am superstrong and can't be hurt by anything. No bad guy in the world is going to want to mess with me. Oh yeah, baby. Daddy, when the bad guys see me coming, they are going to run, run, run. All I got to do is just show up, and I will always be able to save the day." Jahvon laughed.

Daddy paused and looked at Jahvon. His stare sent a chill down Jahvon's spine. After about thirty seconds, Daddy broke his silence. *"Really?"* he said. "Is that a fact?"

Jahvon could sense the mood that Daddy was in at that moment. It was one of the utmost seriousness. It was clear that Jahvon's boasts did not make Daddy happy.

Daddy then said, "So you think you are big and bad because you have all this superpower, huh? You think you're all big and bad because bullets can't hurt you, and you can fall from great heights and not get hurt. *Right?* In fact, you're practically indestructible, so you got nothing to ever worry about from any bad guy, right?"

Jahvon started to feel a bit nervous. Waiting for his main point, he answered all of Daddy's sarcastic questions with an unsure, "Uh, yes."

"So tell me, son, what are you going to do when you face an enemy and your superstrength means nothing? What are you going to do when you face an enemy that laughs at your power? What are you going to do then? Go in the corner and cry like a baby?"

Not thinking before this moment that such a situation was possible, Jahvon had no answer.

Daddy continued, "No matter how powerful and strong you are, there is always something more powerful and stronger. Your most dangerous weapon is not your superpowers. *Your greatest weapon is your mind.* You are not just some dumb brute, son. *You are smart.* Whether you are facing a bad guy or any problem in life, don't just count on your powers." Daddy then affectionately put his left hand on Jahvon's head and gave it a gentle shake. "Use your head. Do understand, son?"

Jahvon responded with a humble, "Yes, Daddy."

Daddy gave an approving kiss on the forehead. He smiled and said, "Good. Now carry these blocks of wood. They're too heavy for me." Then the father and son laughed and joked, talking about football on the way back to the cabin.

Next Joshua had to be tested.

First Daddy took a broken broomstick and just tried to hit Joshua. Over and over again, Daddy swung and missed. Joshua was just too fast. Then Daddy threw rocks at him. Joshua dodged them all easily. Next Daddy, me, and Jahvon tried hitting Joshua with rocks. Joshua easily dodged them all. Then things got interesting...and scary.

Daddy took out his gun. We all wondered why he did that. After all, only Jahvon was bulletproof. Only Jahvon was practically indestructible. Daddy then told Jahvon and me to stand behind him. He instructed Joshua to stand about twenty yards away. My brothers and I grew more scared, especially for Joshua. Daddy then said something that we could not believe.

"Joshua, you have superspeed. There are two types of speed, the evading kind and the north-south kind. Right now we are going to work on the evading kind. I am going to shoot this gun at you." My brothers and I were shocked. We thought, *Well, what if Joshua is not able to dodge a speeding bullet from a highly trained marksman like Daddy? Then our brother will be dead.* Joshua was nervous, too. I could see his skinny legs shaking from twenty yards away.

Daddy could see Joshua was nervous. We were all scared. Jahvon and I spoke up. We pleaded with him that this was not a good idea.

Daddy in anger yelled, "Be quiet, all of you. Do you think I like doing this? But one day you all will face evil. Evil the likes of which you would not believe. I have to do everything I can to make you as prepared for that day as possible."

After Daddy yelled, we were all silent. For Daddy to be so emotional, the evil that he was referencing had to be real.

Then he looked directly at Joshua, making eye contact, and said, "I know, Joshua, that you're scared. But you...can...do...it. I am not asking you to outrun a bullet. I am asking you to dodge a bullet. Let the world slow down around you, and you will dodge whatever comes out of this gun. Do you understand, son?"

Joshua nervously said, "Yes, Daddy."

Joshua was scared. We all were. But we knew that Daddy loved us, and we trusted him. If he said we could do something, then it had to be true.

Daddy said, "OK, Joshua, I am going to count to three. When I get to three I am going to pull the trigger. You...are...going...to...dodge...the...bullet. Do you understand?"

Joshua took a deep breath and said, "Yes, Daddy. I understand."

"Good. Now here we go." Daddy then did something that surprised us. Daddy dropped to one knee and closed his eyes. He said something quietly to himself that only Jahvon and I could hear; Joshua was too far away. Daddy was praying.

He said, "Dear Lord, please don't let me kill my son. Please enable him to dodge the bullet."

Then Daddy stood up and took a deep breath himself. In reality he was just as nervous as the rest of us.

Daddy lifted the gun. He had his right foot behind his left foot. He held the gun in both hands and aimed it directly at the center of Joshua.

Daddy began to yell out the countdown, "One...two...three." He pulled the trigger. There was a loud *pow* sound.

Joshua indeed was able to slow the world down around him. He was actually able to see the bullet coming at him. As the bullet got within five feet of him, Joshua sidestepped it. The bullet went past him and hit a tree.

For me, Daddy, and Jahvon, it appeared as if Joshua had moved like a bolt of lightning as we heard the bang.

We all took a collective deep breath that Daddy had not killed Joshua. "Whew."

Joshua was overjoyed and ran to Daddy to give him a big hug. Daddy with a big smile hugged him back and said, "Good job, son, I am proud of you. *You did it.*"

Jahvon and I gave Joshua a high five. Then something unexpected happened. Joshua had a very eye-opening request for Daddy.

Joshua said, "Do it again, Daddy. Do it again. Shoot at me again. Please, please, please. It was fun. Please!" Joshua was jumping up and down next to daddy with great euphoric excitement at what he had done and what he believed he could do.

Daddy said, "You got it, son."

Daddy had Joshua go back twenty yards. He took out his gun and fired again. Daddy emptied clip after clip of bullets. Each and every bullet missed Joshua. Then Daddy took out two guns. Holding a gun in each hand, Daddy fired both of them at the same time. Again Joshua dodged every bullet. Next Daddy took out a machine gun, an Uzi, and fired it at Joshua. Again Joshua dodged each and every bullet. Finally, for the last test, Daddy took out two Uzis and gave one of them to Jahvon. Daddy knew that Jahvon was strong enough that the machine gun would not fly out of his hand. First he taught Jahvon how to fire the Uzi. Then both he and my father fired the Uzis at the same time. Again, Joshua dodged every bullet that was fired at him.

After hundreds of rounds fired, the bullet-dodging tests were over. We all celebrated. Daddy gave Joshua a big kiss and hug. Jahvon and I also gave Joshua a big hug. We were all very proud of him. Most of all we were happy Joshua was still alive.

The following day, Daddy had another test for Joshua. He wanted to test Joshua's speed running in a straight line. This is what is commonly called "north to south" running.

Daddy had Jahvon and me get into the truck. He told Joshua to race him to a road that was about a mile away.

Daddy said, "On your mark, get set, go!" Daddy pressed the gas pedal to the floor. Joshua took off. Daddy went forty, fifty, sixty, seventy, and then eighty, and then ninety miles per hour. Joshua was keeping up. Finally daddy went over one hundred miles per hour in the truck. That is when Joshua was unable to keep up. Ninety miles per hour was his top speed.

Daddy had a talk with Joshua about his running. "Son, running is not just about talent; it's also about technique. You run in a wild manner. You need more control. Remember, the harder you pump your arms, the faster you will go. Also try breathing in through your nose and out through your mouth when you are trying to go as fast as you can."

Daddy also wanted to measure Joshua's endurance. So he had Joshua run along the side of the truck. But after a short period of time, Joshua would collapse on the dirt road out of pure exhaustion. The whole family would run from the truck to check on him. His chest would be pounding, and he would be gasping for air.

Even after Daddy made the changes to his running technique, Joshua tired quickly. This made Daddy nervous. If Joshua were one day being chased down by bad guys, they would get him if they were fast themselves and did not get tired.

Daddy knew that to help Joshua with this endurance problem would require more than just cardio training. He decided to test Joshua's hand-to-hand combat skills.

Daddy was himself a black belt in karate. He also had some knowledge of other martial arts. He taught us all some basic moves. However, Joshua learned the most quickly. He performed every technique even better than Daddy. In addition to his superspeed, Joshua had photographic recall. He could watch someone do something and then do it with equal skill. This included acrobatic flips like a gymnast as well as martial arts techniques. Daddy, Jahvon, and I marveled at Joshua's athletic ability. His agility and skill were truly incredible to behold. With his combined athleticism and superspeed, there was no way anyone could defeat him in hand-to-hand combat. Unless, of course, they had superstrength like Jahvon.

However, Joshua still lacked endurance. One day during a workout, my father had a one-on-one talk with him.

Daddy said, "You have a lot of great skill and speed."

Joshua, feeling very proud and always wanting Dad's approval, said, "Thanks, Daddy."

"Tell me, son, what is the most important thing in the martial arts?"

The question confused Joshua, but he tried to answer. "Is it punching? Kicking? Joint locks? Throws? What is it, Daddy?" Joshua was excited to hear the answer.

Daddy put his right hand on Joshua's shoulder, smiled, and said, "Breathing."

Joshua's response was a confused *Huh?* "So in a fight, am I supposed to breathe on a bad guy and knock him out with my breath, Daddy?" Joshua laughed. "That sounds more like something Jahvon can do."

Jahvon from a distance yelled, "I heard that."

Daddy smiled then calmly said, "No, that is not what I mean. Breathing is how a person regulates and develops his internal energy. You can't do anything if you can't breathe. No matter how athletic you are, you cannot be a great martial artist if you do not know how to breathe. And the breathing that will help you become a great martial artist will also help you in your running."

Joshua, still confused, asked, "How, Daddy?"

"You have to be able to control your breathing and your heart rate, and this means controlling your mind and your thoughts. Then, when you are running and out of breath, you will be able to get your second wind. Your second wind lets you keep running when you feel you can't run any more. Learning *katas* will help you do this.

Katas, in the martial arts, are a series of movements. I am going to show you some katas that will help you to calm your mind and control your breathing."

Daddy then showed Joshua some katas that he knew. He did not want Joshua to focus on just the physical movements but to concentrate on controlling his breathing while doing each kata movement. Jahvon and I watched as Joshua and Daddy simultaneously did different martial arts katas. Daddy told Joshua to control his breathing and calm his mind, to block out everything around him and focus on slowing down his heartbeat.

We did not have much time in the Poconos. So Daddy focused on training us in the areas that he felt was the most important. Because of Joshua's abilities and weaknesses, he taught the katas only to him. At a later date either he or Joshua could teach them to Jahvon and me.

Thanks to Daddy's teachings, my brothers learned more about themselves and what they could do. But being in the Poconos was not all business for us. We also had a good time. We played games, talked, and laughed. We were already a close family. Being together in the mountains allowed to us to get even closer.

My power was that I was just really smart. I knew a lot about a lot of things. My mind moved fast. I had a great mastery of all the sciences. Even the most advanced problem was easy for me. I was able to build anything I wanted if I had the right tools. Daddy did not have me display my power and evaluate me the way he did my brothers. His teaching came unexpectedly. It came not with drills but with a simple father-and-son talk. Daddy and I sat on the grass together on a beautiful sunny day. We were watching Jahvon and Joshua in the distance playing catch with the football. Jahvon would use his strength and throw the ball really far, while Joshua would use his speed to run underneath the ball and catch it.

I sighed and said, "Daddy, why couldn't I have had the superstrength or the superspeed? I'm just good with numbers and I can process information. *Big deal.* I am just one big brain. A *nerd.*"

Daddy put his right hand on my shoulder and gave me a gentle, reassuring shake. He smiled and said, "So you're jealous of your brothers, huh?"

I gave him a sad nod.

"Put your hand on your chest," he said. "What do you feel?"

I thought that was a very strange question. "Um, my heartbeat."

He pointed to birds in the sky flying in an arrow formation. "What do you see, son?"

"I see birds flying in an arrow formation?"

He pointed at some trees and asked, "What do you see over there, son?"

"I see some trees, Daddy."

"What do you see up there?" He was pointing at the clouds in the sky.

I said, "Um, Daddy, I see clouds."

I wondered why Daddy was asking me all these silly questions. When he told me, the answer was so obvious that, even with my genius intellect, I did not realize that I was being taught a valuable lesson—a lesson I would always remember.

His eyes widened, and he said, "Everything you see, everything you touch, feel, or hear *it's all mathematics*. It does not matter if it's the waves of the ocean or the power of the sun. It does not matter if it's the millions of cells in your body, the grass, trees, people, roads, birds, or clouds in the sky; it's all mathematics, son. Everything in the universe is mathematics. You are a master of mathematics. That means there is nothing you can't do. You're jealous of your brothers? You got it wrong, son. It's your brothers who should be jealous of you."

I was blown away. What he said was so true. I felt better. I felt reassured about myself. Although I still had my doubts. "Daddy, what if I am in a situation where I am under pressure to figure out something and maybe...maybe lives are at stake, and I am too scared or nervous to concentrate? People could die. And it will be because of me failing."

He took a deep breath and stood up. He asked me to please stand up. He gave me a hug and a kiss on the forehead. Then he looked at me and said in a firm but loving tone, "Son, in life there are bad things and bad people. They will do everything they can to distract you from doing the thing that you need to do when you need to do it. You have to be able to fight through that. When the time is right, you must be able to focus like a laser—like a laser, son—on what you are doing. During that time you have to block out from your mind any and all negativity while you're doing whatever it is you're doing."

I responded with a desperate, "How, Daddy? How?"

Daddy told me to close my eyes. Then he said to lift my arms up to the side and tilt my head back. He told me to take a deep breath. Inhale through my nose and exhale through my mouth. I did as he asked.

"Use your imagination, son. Feel yourself becoming one with the universe."

At that moment I thought Daddy was crazy.

"Now repeat after me," he said. "I am the universe."

"I am the universe," I said.

"The universe is me."

"The universe is me."

"I am mathematics," he said.

"I am mathematics."

"Mathematics is me."

I repeated it: "Mathematics is me." Somehow at that moment I felt better. I felt…more *confident*.

"When you are trying to do something, son, use this saying as way to help you get through it. Your biggest problem is your confidence. Once you overcome that, then you can do anything. And, remember, I love you now and forever."

I felt better. I gave Daddy a big hug and said, "Thanks, Daddy."

"Welcome, son."

***

We were in Mr. Ferrante's cabin for about ten days. It was almost time for us to head back to New York. After Daddy gave us all our own individualized training and wisdom on life, we spent most of our time enjoying ourselves. We played sports. We even jumped into a lake. Well, at least most of us did. Jahvon, because of his density, sank like a stone. Swimming was not his thing. Although Jahvon was practically indestructible, he still needed to breathe. His one weakness was that he could drown. So Daddy kept him away from the water. Joshua and I did not do any swimming once we knew of the danger it posed to our brother. We did not want to do anything that did not include him. My dad appreciated that solidarity.

The night before our last night in the cabin, Daddy did something that he did not want to do but that he knew he must: He told my brothers and me the truth about the past. Before he would tell us only bits and pieces of the past. He did not think we were ready for the whole truth. He still was unsure we were ready, but he had this uneasiness about the future. Somehow he could sense that his time with us was not going to last much longer. Telling us the truth about the past was his way of helping us be more prepared for the future.

It was a quiet, calm night. We had just finished having dinner. The fireplace was burning. Daddy had us all gather around him. Then, in a very somber tone, he told us everything. He told us about what had happened to him and his unit in Syria. He told us about our creator, Nicholas Hammerstein. He told us about Ajax and what he and the Creator had done to him. He told us how we were created, and why we were created. He told us about the three children created before us and how they had been discarded in the trash. He told us how he had hid with us in the woods. He told us about the man in North Carolina who had helped him, about being on the run, and stealing to survive. He told us everything.

Hearing it was tough for us. All this time we had thought we had a mother like other kids, but that Daddy, for whatever reason, had decided not to talk about her. To find out that we had never had a mother was hard. To find out that we were creations of an evil madman for an evil purpose was even harder. To hear that we had been created to become killers, like three

Frankenstein's monsters, was unbelievable for us. But, as tough as it was, it all made sense. We could do things that no one else could do. How else could this have happened, other than this tale of horror and survival that our father was now telling us? We cried. Nothing hurts like the truth, and at this moment we were hurting.

But like a mighty anchor for a ship knocked around by powerful waves, Daddy kept us grounded and stable emotionally. He said something that helped us hear the truth. He gave us inspiration that we really needed in that moment. He did it with his words. He said something that we would never forget in a powerful reassuring voice.

Daddy said, "You were created by evil, but you shall work for good. You were created to hurt people, but you shall help people. You were meant to be prodigies of death, destruction, and despair in the world, but you shall give the world hope when it seems all hope is lost. You are indeed prodigies. But you are prodigies of making the world a better place. And you are my sons. I am proud of you, and I love you. Never forget that." We all looked at him and ran into his arms sobbing. He embraced the three of us at the same time. He held us as we cried for about five minutes.

We each told him, "Love you, too, Daddy." Then he tucked us each in our beds and wished us a good night.

Finally we left the Poconos and Mr. Ferrante's cabin. We'd had a good time overall, and we learned more about who we were and what we could do. As we traveled back to New York with the sobering knowledge of our past, we each felt a sense of responsibility and obligation to use our powers to help people, just as our father said. Also our love for our father was even greater. We had a greater appreciation for him and all he had done for us. Perhaps the biggest thing he'd done was to prevent us from growing up to become monsters like our Creator.

My brothers and I planned on baking our daddy a "We love and appreciate you, Daddy" cake when we got back to New York. We kept this a secret from Daddy. We wanted to surprise him.

***

When we got back to New York, we unpacked and got settled. Daddy thanked Mr. Ferrante for letting us use his cabin in the Poconos. Daddy got ready to get back to work. In the meantime I began putting my cake together. I was going to make sure it was one that Daddy would never forget. Jahvon and Joshua were excited to help me bake it.

A few days after our return from the Poconos, the special cake for Daddy was ready. Daddy came home tired from working in the kitchen for twelve hours. My brothers and I, smiles on our faces, surrounded him as he came through the door. We asked Daddy to not move. Then we told him we had surprise for him. Daddy, though tired and wanting to just sit down and watch TV, complied with our wish and didn't move. I took out a device and pressed a few buttons. My daddy's jaw almost fell to floor. I had placed minirockets under a platter from the kitchen downstairs. On the platter stood a huge, vanilla pound-cheesecake. Pound cake and cheesecake were Daddy's favorite cakes. So I'd combined them into one great-tasting cake. On top of the cake I had written in frosting, "We love you, Daddy."

But what was most special about the cake was the fact that it was flying in the air, thanks to the minirockets that I'd made. This big cake hovered four feet above the ground. It had candles. I controlled the flight of the cake to hover by Daddy. I built in a small fireworks show. The candles I made exploded like the fireworks that one would see during the Fourth of July. When the fireworks exploded, they created the message, "We love you, Daddy." Then another firework went off and exploded from the candles, spelling out, "You rock, Daddy." Then a third wrote, "Daddy, you're the best." The fireworks were small and extinguished in the air in our living room almost as quickly as they appeared. There was no risk of an accidental fire occurring. Daddy was in awe to see a flying cake with mini fireworks. He then blew the candles out. We all cheered.

Then my brothers and I started chanting, "Daddy, Daddy, Daddy." Jahvon picked Daddy up and put him on his shoulders. We all kept chanting, "Daddy, Daddy." Jahvon danced and bounced with Daddy on his shoulders. Daddy had a huge smile on his face, and he was laughing. He was enjoying our surprise. Joshua jumped in the air and flipped, and as he was flipping he gave Daddy a high five. I finally handed Daddy a cutting knife while he was on Jahvon's shoulders. Jahvon stopped hopping and dancing. I then had the cake hover up to Daddy. While the cake was in midair, Daddy cut a slice. He then put it in his hand and ate that slice.

With cake all over his lips, Daddy said, "Mm, it's good. Thanks, boys. You guys are the best."

Joshua said, "You are the best too, Daddy."

So that night we laughed and ate cake. I, of course, baked a whole separate cake of the same size just for Joshua, to accommodate his incredible appetite.

Daddy was really happy and could not stop smiling. Our surprise was a success. He asked me what the special occasion for the cake was.

"You don't always have to have a special occasion to let the ones you love know that you love and appreciate them," I said.

Daddy hugged me and smiled and said emotionally, "So true."

Then we got ready for bed. In all the excitement we did not realize that Daddy had something in a bag. It was a video camera with a tripod stand.

While my brothers and I were taking our showers and brushing our teeth, Daddy set up the camera in his bedroom and closed his door. Whatever he was going to do, he wanted to be alone. But the door was still open a crack, enough that I could see that Daddy had turned on the camera and got on his knees. He then began talking to the camera. The camera was recording. I could not hear what he was saying due to the television in the living room and the noise my brothers were making in the background. However, I could see that Daddy looked sad. I wondered what could make Daddy look sad after such a fun night of cake and laughter. I did not have any answers.

Before my father finished with his message, my brothers came storming into his bedroom. They wanted to say good night. We never went to bed without giving Daddy a hug and kiss and saying good night. So Jahvon and Joshua each gave Daddy a hug and kiss. They were sleepy and had stomachs filled with cake. They just wanted to go lie down. They were not curious in the slightest as to what Daddy was doing.

After they left the room and went to bed, I walked in. I also gave Daddy and hug and kiss. But, instead of saying good night, I asked, "What are you doing, Daddy?"

With a sad look, he turned to the camera that was still recording. He said in a sad voice, "I'm just saying hi to an old friend." He pulled my head toward him and kissed me on the forehead. "Now go get some sleep."

As I left his room, I could not help but turn around.

Daddy was kneeling in front of the camera, his right hand raised in an inverted fist—thumb facing the ceiling and pinky facing the ground. He gave a slight pump in the air, as if to a person who was not there. Then he turned the recording off.

I went to bed curious who that person might be. Little did I know that I would find out in the not-too-distant future.

Chapter 11

Save the Hostages

A month after we got back from the Poconos, Mr. Ferrante asked my father to do something that he really did not want to do. Mr. Ferrante had to take care of some business with his bank downtown. He wanted Daddy to drive him there. Parking in downtown Brooklyn was next to impossible. It was much easier to have someone drop you off and then pick you up when you'd finished your business. My dad did not like the idea of going downtown because of all the security cameras. Downtown Brooklyn had almost as many cameras as downtown Manhattan. My father was always fearful of being seen by the Dawn of the Shadow. He was always worried that they might be networked into a camera system somewhere.

My dad told Mr. Ferrante that everything was electronic nowadays. He did not need to go into a bank branch. He could do all his banking on the Internet.

Mr. Ferrante had an interesting response. "Jordan, I am what the kids call 'old school.' I like doing business face-to-face. Now, I need you to drive me there. So are you going to do it or what?" My father could not refuse a man who had been so good to him and his family for so many years. So he agreed to do it.

Dad came upstairs from the kitchen where he and Mr. Ferrante were talking. He told us what he was going to do. He put on a hoodie and a cap to hide his face as much as he could. Then he and Mr. Ferrante got into the Ford SUV. Daddy drove while Mr. Ferrante sat in the front passenger seat. Mr. Ferrante was in a great mood. He was enjoying all the new revenues from the sales of the pasta sauce I'd created, plus the additional traffic at his restaurants. Mr. Ferrante was looking to expand his business even further. So he was going to the bank to get a business loan to help finance his expansions. Mr. Ferrante never stopped trying to convince my father to be partners with him. He really wanted my dad to share in all his success. After all, it was his son who created the pasta sauce. My father was grateful but refused. As always, he wanted to lay low.

When my dad and Mr. Ferrante got into downtown, they were fortunate to find a parking spot. Parking spots downtown were indeed a rare thing. Mr. Ferrante got out of the car and asked my dad to come in with him. Mr. Ferrante wanted to do some shopping afterward, and he wanted my father's company. Mr. Ferrante looked upon my father almost like a son and always enjoyed his company. Daddy reluctantly got out of the car and joined Mr. Ferrante in the bank. My dad kept his hoodie and cap on and his head down. This was to make sure that no cameras would get a clear image of his face.

My father and Mr. Ferrante sat on the couch in the bank and waited to be seen by a representative. This was a huge bank. The entire building of ten stories belonged to the bank. The first floor lobby had huge glass windows where people could see in and out. Cameras were everywhere.

It seemed like a nice, quiet day, and nothing seemed unusual. My father still felt uneasy. Perhaps it was from his time going on missions as a Navy SEAL. Perhaps he knew that there was a madman and evil terrorist organization looking for him. He just knew at that moment something felt wrong.

Then, when it was Mr. Ferrante's turn to see a representative, thirty armed gunmen came running into the bank. They seemed to appear out of nowhere. Black masks covered their mouths and showed only the tops of their faces. They carried high-powered firearms that Daddy recognized as military weapons.

The armed men shot and killed the two police officers standing guard in the bank. The police did not have a chance. Then, perhaps to show the people in the lobby that they meant business, the intruders shot and killed two of the bank staff. The customers screamed. Women clutched their children. Others begged the armed men to not hurt them.

One of the armed men yelled in an Arabic accent, "Do as we tell you, or we will blow your damn heads off. Now everyone get to the stairs in the back of the lobby. Move, move, move!" Two more men carrying a big trunk ran from a black van into the building. The armed men marched all one hundred or so people up the stairs at the back of the lobby. This included Daddy and Mr. Ferrante. Mr. Ferrante was somewhat old and a chubby man. My father held him by his arm to give him support. The people were scrambling and hustling as best they could to follow the orders. In the stampede, people stumbled and desperately hurried to get back up. Daddy, still holding on to Mr. Ferrante, made sure that Mr. Ferrante kept pace.

The crowd was herded like cattle to the third floor, where they were led down a long corridor to a huge auditorium. The men carrying the trunk placed it on a stage at the front of the auditorium. When they opened the trunk, my father was not surprised at what he saw. It was clearly a bomb of some sort.

The armed men were spread throughout the building. There were four in the auditorium with Daddy and the other hostages and six in the lobby. The others were on the staircases and the rooftops.

The men in the lobby knew that the police would be coming, and when the police charged into the bank, a ferocious firefight left five more officers dead. Then the men activated a smoke device in the lobby. This way the people outside could not see in.

The police made a perimeter around the area and moved everyone off the sidewalks. SWAT teams deployed to the roofs of the surrounding buildings. Police helicopters took to the air. Outside the perimeter, huge crowds gathered. This crowd included the media.

***

My brothers and I were watching television when all of a sudden there was "breaking news." The media showed how a hostage situation at the Bank de Gente. This was the very same bank that Daddy was going to with Mr. Ferrante. I immediately called Daddy on the cheap cell phone that he never used. He just had it for emergencies. I got no answer. Then I texted him. Daddy must have somehow managed to turn off his ringer as he was being herded with the other hostages.

My brothers and I were pacing up and down our apartment, frantic.

Jahvon kept yelling, "The bad guys have Daddy. The bad guys have Daddy."

Then Joshua yelled, "We need to go beat up the bad guys and save Daddy."

Jahvon quickly responded, "Yeah, we need to beat those bad guys up and save Daddy."

I was trying to remain calm. I tried to calm them down even though my instinct was in agreement with them.

I said, "Look, guys, we don't even know if the bad guys have Daddy. After all, Daddy may have gotten out of the bank before these terrorists showed up."

Then I got a text that destroyed that hopeful theory. The text was from Daddy's phone. It read, "I am one of the hostages in the bank. Do not try to rescue me." Daddy knew there was no way for my brothers and I to rescue him and take on the terrorists without exposing our powers to the world, as well as revealing our location to the Dawn of the Shadow. Between all the media coverage and all the cameras, Hammerstein would find us. That was a risk that Daddy did not want us to take.

I showed the text to my brothers. They could not believe it.

Jahvon was furious. He shouted, "We can take these bad guys and save the day."

"That's right. We can beat these bad guys up," Joshua said.

I was in full agreement with my brothers. But our father's commands were our law.

Then one of the news reporters stated that there had been gunfire and that witnesses had seen people getting shot.

That changed my mind. I made a decision. The decision was to go against what Daddy said and to follow our instincts. I told my brothers my decision, and they agreed. I then I took a deep breath before I sent a text back to Daddy. I knew he would not be pleased.

My text in caps said, "SORRY, DADDY BUT WE ARE COMING TO SAVE YOU. I KNOW WE ARE DISOBEYING YOU. YOU CAN PUNISH US AFTER WE SAVE YOU. OK? LOVE YOU, JASON." We waited for about 120 seconds to see if Daddy would respond. Finally, he did.

His text said, "There are thirty armed gunman. They have me and the other hostages on the third floor in a big auditorium. They also have an exploding device in the auditorium. Not only will you have to deal with the terrorists, but you are going to have to find a way past the police. Be careful. Love you back. Daddy." My father realized that he was in no position to stop us. So he gave us as much information as he could to help us save the day.

My brothers were excited. They could not wait to take on hardcore bad guys and flex their muscles. Especially Jahvon.

So I made a plan, and then we got together in our living room and made a huddle. Much like how a football or basketball team will do before a game. Jahvon gave us some words to pump us up.

He said, "All right, we are going to beat up these bad guys and save Daddy and the hostages. Right?"

Joshua and I yelled simultaneously, "Right!"

Then Joshua said, "Family on three. One..." Joshua stuck his hand out.

Then Jahvon yelled, "Two..." and stuck his hand on top of Joshua's.

I finished with a loud, "Three!" and placed my hand on top of my brothers'.

Then we all yelled at the same time, "Family!" and hugged one another. Now we were pumped to save the day.

First we needed a disguise so no one could identify us. We took three of our T-shirts and put holes in them and wrapped them around our heads to hide our faces. The holes were for our eyes so we could see. We looked like bandits. Now we needed transportation. We went into the back of the building. There were always a lot of cars driving by. Joshua ran into the middle of the street and waved down a Yellow Cab. The cabbie stopped his car in front of Joshua and yelled at him to get out of the street. That is when Jahvon walked up to the side of the taxi and reached inside the window and pulled the cab driver out. The cabbie was in disbelief that some masked kid had the strength to pull him out of the cab.

The cabbie let out a groan as Jahvon tossed him on the sidewalk. The cab driver just had a couple of bruises from being tossed eight feet after being pulled out of the cab.

Jahvon looked at the cabbie on the ground and yelled, "Sorry, this is a matter of national security." We all then loaded in the cab. I took the driver's seat.

Joshua asked me, "You can drive this?"

I responded confidently, "I can drive anything." We took off to the bank, determined to save the day.

In the cab we were only able to get so far. This was due to the perimeter blockade by the police. We had to get past it somehow.

I pulled the cab up to a police car where two big athletic-looking male police officers were. We walked up to the police, who tried to get us to go away.

Jahvon said, "Um, sorry about the headache, officers."

One of the cops laughed and asked, "What headache, boy?"

Jahvon gently said, "Um, this one."

Jahvon grabbed the cops by their belts and lifted them both up, cracking the heads of the two cops together. This was enough to knock the cops out. We took the keys to their squad car.

Jahvon looked at the cop who'd called him "boy" and said to the now-knocked-out police officer, "Don't call me 'boy.'" Despite Jahvon's statement, we felt bad that we had to beat up cops and steal cars. But we were not going to let anything stop us from rescuing our dad.

Back inside the bank, the terrorists were feeling good about what they had done. No one could stop them. The smoke in the lobby meant the police snipers could not fire into the bank; they could not see where the bad guys were. The police were at a standstill.

Meanwhile the terrorists were trying to carry out a large-scale suicide mission. They intended to explode the bomb and kill as many people as possible. The only better place to do it than downtown Manhattan was in downtown Brooklyn because it was considered another prestigious area in the United States.

The police closest to the bank had their guns drawn and pointing at the bank. They were waiting for orders as to how to proceed. The FBI was coming to the scene.

The sound of police sirens going off stunned everyone in the area. The police themselves were shocked because they had not ordered this. The terrorists saw the police car coming from the windows above.

One of the armed gunmen yelled in Arabic on his communication device, "A police car is coming at top speed into the lobby. Get ready." Then ten of the thirty armed men positioned themselves in the lobby in the bank. They had guns drawn and were waiting for the police car to come crashing into the lobby. The police car did indeed come crashing through the lobby. It came in through the side of the bank, right through the wall and a huge glass window. There was a loud shattering noise, and the ten armed gunmen in the lobby opened fire, shooting hundreds of rounds at the police car.

Then one of the armed men yelled in Arabic, "Cease fire."

The armed men all felt the same uneasy feeling that something was not right. One of the armed men walked up to the police car. At first he did not see anyone in the car. Not even in the driver's seat. Then the armed man got up close to the driver-side window. He was shocked by what he saw. He saw Jahvon lying on the front seat with his upper body near the passenger window.

Jahvon looked at the armed man and smiled and said, "Hello."

The armed man wondered how could a kid survive hundreds of rounds of bullets. Too bad for him, he was not going to get an answer at that moment. Jahvon lifted his knees toward his chest and kicked out the driver-side door of the squad car. Jahvon did this with such force that the door flew into the armed man and sent him sailing into the wall behind him. He fell to the floor unconscious. *One bad guy down, twenty-nine to go,* Jahvon thought. He hurried out of the squad car, and the other nine armed men started shooting at him. Unfortunately for them, they were facing a prodigy.

The bullets bounced right off of Jahvon. Even the bullets to his head did not bother him. The armed men kept firing; they could not believe what they saw. Jahvon went up to one of the armed men and backhanded him with his left arm. He struck the armed gunman with such force that he flew ten feet into another armed man behind him, knocking them both out. *Now three down and twenty-seven to go,* Jahvon thought.

One of the armed men came up from behind Jahvon with an axe. He swung it at Jahvon's neck. Upon impact the axe broke.

The armed men were starting to feel fear. Fear of a twelve-year-old.

Jahvon grabbed that terrorist who'd just tried to chop his head off. "Let me introduce you to the law of gravity. What goes up..." he said and threw the terrorist so hard into the air that he hit the twenty-foot-high ceiling and was knocked out. "Well, you know the rest," Jahvon said, and the man's unconscious body fell to the floor.

Four down, twenty-six to go, and I have not even broken a sweat.

That was when Joshua and I got out of the trunk of the car. I knew that the bad guys would fire upon the squad car if it came crashing into the bank. I also knew that all the firepower would be concentrated on the driver's seat and the front of the car. Not the trunk. So all Jahvon had to do was press down on the gas with the car pointed toward the bank and, *voila*, we would be in the bank.

Joshua quickly ran up to Jahvon with an angry look and said, "Hey, leave some bad guys for me." Then Joshua picked up a baton from one of the police who had been killed earlier. With his superspeed and skill in Escrima—a Filipino martial art that specializes in hand-to-hand combat with sticks—he ran to the remaining six gunmen in the lobby. He struck them each in their knees, causing them to buckle. Then he cracked them over their heads, knocking them out.

Now there were ten bad guys down and twenty to go.

After my brothers took out the ten terrorists in the lobby, a sound came from one of the unconscious men. It was the voice of one of the other terrorists from another part of the bank, calling to find out what was going on in the lobby.

I picked up the device and said in Arabic, "Everything is fine here and under control. We do need more men just to help further secure the lobby in case the police try another attack."

The person on the other end responded, "OK." Then we heard footsteps coming down the stairs. Another group of ten armed men rushed into the lobby, two at a time. They were shocked to see all their comrades on the floor, unconscious. Joshua took the fire hose and wrapped them up with it. He tied a knot in the hose and, with blinding speed, passed the other end to Jahvon, who took the hose in both hands and pulled it with such force that all ten men went flying into the air, yelling. They slammed into the lobby wall so hard that four were instantly knocked out. Joshua ran up to those still conscious and hit them each over the head with the baton, knocking them out.

Twenty bad guys down and ten to go.

Meanwhile, in the auditorium, the terrorists had pressed a number of buttons on the explosive device. My father recognized the material for the bomb. It was C-4, an explosive material used by the military. Enough to destroy the whole block, killing perhaps over a thousand people.

Then the terrorists did something surprising. They took another device out. It looked almost like a cell phone. They pushed a couple of buttons, and a yellow glowing energy surrounded the bomb. The terrorists were very pleased with themselves.

My father wondered why the terrorists would put some type of field over the bomb. It would defeat the purpose of allowing the bomb to explode outward. Then he put it all together. He saw that the bomb had a timer of ten minutes. He also saw another timer. This timer must have been for the device creating the glowing energy. It had a timer of nine minutes and forty seconds. The terrorists were making sure that no one, such as the police bomb squad, could try to deactivate the bomb. That was the purpose of the glowing energy field; it would switch off right before the bomb exploded. Even the best bomb squad would need more than twenty seconds to deactivate the bomb.

My brothers and I ran upstairs to the third-floor landing. Joshua got there first because of his speed. On the landing were two of the armed men. They pointed their weapons at us, but with two quick kicks Joshua knocked the guns out of their hands. Then with an unbelievably fast and fluid motion, Joshua grabbed one of the guns as it flew through the air. He used the steel butt of the gun and smashed the two terrorists in the head. *Bap, bap*!

Twenty-two bad guys down, only eight to go.

Six more armed men saw their comrades taken out and began firing at Joshua and me. We both ran for cover and got to one side of the staircase. The bullets could not reach us, but nor could we enter the hall. Joshua was not ready to test his ability to dodge bullets against these four terrorists. I did not blame him.

Joshua yelled, "Where the heck is Jahvon?"

Then, with a mighty *boom*, Jahvon jumped from the hallway on the second floor through the ceiling. This put him on the third-floor hallway, right in the middle of the four terrorists that were shooting at us. The terrorists turned and fired on Jahvon. The bullets, like earlier, just bounced off him. Jahvon grabbed the two bad guys closest to him. One bad guy in each hand. With his great strength, as he had done to the cops earlier, he lifted them both over his head, knocking their heads together.

Two more bad guys down, now only six left.

Then one of the terrorists took out a flamethrower. He blasted Jahvon with it. It did not hurt Jahvon, but it did burn his clothes. Joshua then ran down the hall to help Jahvon, not that Jahvon needed it. Joshua jumped over the hole that Jahvon had made in the floor, ran behind the terrorist with the flamethrower, and kicked him in the groin.

The terrorist bent over and yelled.

Jahvon said, "Ooh, man, that had to hurt."

Then Joshua finished off the terrorist with a gun butt to the back of the head.

The last terrorist in the hall, in shock at seeing these superhuman kids, ran back toward the auditorium. However, Joshua was too fast and tripped him from behind. Then Joshua banged him over the head with the butt of the gun.

Now there were only two terrorists left.

Daddy and the hostages heard the fighting from the auditorium. He figured that had to be us, and he started slowly moving toward one of the two terrorists in the auditorium. The other one ran out to the hall to try to help his comrades. As he reached the door, it was knocked off its hinges by a punch from Jahvon. The blow was so powerful it sent the steel door flying five feet into the terrorist, knocking him out.

The last terrorist and everyone else in the auditorium were shocked by what they had just seen. Everyone except my father. He took advantage of the moment and grabbed the terrorist's gun with his left hand. Then, with his right hand, he punched the terrorist in the jaw, knocking him out cold. My brothers and I saw what

Daddy did and smiled proudly. Joshua laughed and yelled, "You got skills, Daddy!"

I quickly went up to Joshua and said, "You idiot, we are not supposed to let anyone know who we are, remember?"

Joshua, feeling a bit embarrassed, hesitantly said, "Um, good job, citizen. Next time leave the bad guys to us."

At that moment my father quickly reminded us that the danger was not over. He yelled at the hostages, "Everyone, this bomb is about to go off. Get out of the building now. Move, people, move!"

The hostages and Mr. Ferrante started toward the auditorium exit. The younger and stronger hostages helped the children and the elderly.

We joined Dad by the bomb.

Dad turned to me and said, "Do you recognize this field, son?"

I did recognize it, and I knew exactly how to deactivate it. It was a type of organic energy that could be destroyed with a combination of heat and cold. I also recognized the bomb and knew that if the bomb went off, it would bring down this whole building. Only Jahvon would survive the blast.

I told Daddy that this field was an exotic, powerful energy field that scientists used for defensive measures in warfare. The field was pretty much indestructible.

My father was not interested in a lecture on the subject at that moment. Time was running out. A lot of people would die if we didn't destroy the energy field and deactivate the bomb.

Jahvon tried to smash it. He gave it two powerful punches, but he did not affect the field at all.

I said, "Brute force will not destroy energy like this." I told Joshua to get the flamethrower.

Joshua quickly ran up to the unconscious terrorist with the flamethrower still in the hall. He took the flamethrower and brought it to me. I then had my father blast the field with fire. As he did, the glow from the energy field turned red. Then I told Joshua to get me one of the fire extinguishers on the wall. Using his superspeed, he got me the fire extinguisher. Now the timer on the bomb was down to two minutes. I blasted the now-red energy field with the coldness of the fire extinguisher. The field turned blue. I took the baton from Joshua and swung it at the blue energy field. The field began to crack. The cracks grew bigger and bigger after each blow until finally the field broke into pieces that dissolved in the air. My family was amazed.

Now I had to deactivate the bomb. There were only thirty seconds left. Even the best bomb squad would need about five minutes to deactivate a bomb that had the sophisticated wires and digital starter that this one had. But I didn't. I entered the proper coding commands to deactivate the device.

Everyone gave a collective sigh of relief that the bomb was no longer a threat. I explained to my family, who were still in awe, that the energy field, as powerful as it was, still had a weakness in two basic elements. They were fire and cold. I knew about this energy from the vast information that I got by studying anything and everything on the Internet over the years and reading every book in every library my father ever took me to. My memory was photographic. I was truly like a living computer. I also had a vast amount of knowledge on explosives and how they worked. This made the deactivation very easy...well, at least easy for me.

My father said, "Great job, boys. Now get out of here. The police will be here soon. I'll see you back at the apartment. Now go." We all gave Daddy a quick hug and left. The police were coming in as the hostages were going out. That was good for us because the hostages slowed the police down. My brothers and I found another staircase that led to the basement of the building. Jahvon smashed a hole in the ground for us, and we ended up in the sewers. We traveled through the sewers for a few blocks. Then we came up into the street through one of the manhole covers. It was disgusting to be in the sewers, but at least we were able to avoid the police. The police were cuffing the terrorists and getting the hostages any medical attention they needed.

The events were all over the news. The hostages were telling the police and reporters of the three kids with masks who stopped the terrorists. Even the terrorists who were arrested were speaking of kids with incredible superpowers. Also there were video cameras in the bank that caught my brothers and me in action against the terrorists.

We finally reunited with our father later that evening back at the house. We were all very happy. Daddy told us how proud he was of us. We took showers and changed our clothes. Then we started high-fiving one another and bragging about how we beat up the bad guys. Joshua boasted about what he did. Then Jahvon talked about what he did. Even I was caught up in this glorious moment. So, of course, I reminded my brothers of when I spoke Arabic and deactivated the energy field and the bomb. I noticed that in our celebration, for some reason, my dad looked a bit nervous and sad. I did not understand why he seemed that way after the family just kicked butt and saved the lives of hundreds if not close to a thousand people. Sadly, the whole family would soon find out what was disturbing my father.

Chapter 12

Reunion of Death

The following day, my father asked us to start packing our bags. We were all surprised. We had just come back not too long ago from a trip to the Poconos. *Where could we be packing up to go to now?* I wondered.

Jahvon asked, "Daddy, why are we packing? Where are we going?"

Daddy told us all to gather around him. He then took a deep breath, paused, and spoke words that were hard for him to say.

He said, "Look, boys, the time has come for us to leave. We are going to live somewhere else. I know you like it here, but it's just not safe for us to be here anymore. I am not sure where we are going to go, but I just know that we can't stay in New York anymore. I am going to get a car and some money from Mr. Ferrante, and we are going to leave first thing in the morning."

We all immediately voiced our complaints.

Then Daddy put his finger to his mouth and said, "Shhh. Boys, I wish this was easy. But you are going to have to trust me. It's for the best, OK?" Daddy's voice shook a little.

The emotion in his voice made us pause. Then we nodded and agreed to start packing.

Daddy did some packing himself. He made sure that the disk that he'd recorded his video message on was safe in his little trunk. Then he gave us all a hug and left us to go talk to Mr. Ferrante, who we were all sure was going to be just as surprised as the rest of us by our father's decision.

After about six hours of watching television and packing, my brothers and I were finally finished. We thought it was odd that Daddy had been gone for so long. I called him on his cell phone and got no answer. I looked out front and noticed that there was no traffic coming into the restaurant. This was on a Saturday afternoon. Normally, that was when the restaurant was busiest. I asked my brothers to turn off the television and the radio and be still. The silence was chilling. Normally, we could hear activity in the kitchen beneath us. We could hear the sound of people gathering. Mr. Ferrante usually had classical music in the background— great vocalists like Andrea Bocelli. Now we heard nothing.

We decided to investigate what was going on. We wanted to know why everything was so quiet. We walked down the stairs and into the kitchen. Once we got into the kitchen, we were horrified by what we saw. All the cooks and kitchen staff were dead. They had been shot. We ran through the kitchen and into the main dining area. We were even more horrified. All the wait staff were dead also. The doors of the restaurant were closed. The killers had put up the Closed sign. That was why people just walked by and did not enter.

We had never seen any kind of massacre like this. Mr. Ferrante's staff had always been friendly to us. We had gotten to know many of them over the years. My brothers and I started to cry. Sure, we had superpowers, but we were still twelve-year-old kids.

Jahvon, with tears in his eyes, yelled, "Where is Daddy and Mr. Ferrante?"

Joshua with his superspeed ran to check outside the back of the restaurant, while Jahvon went to check the public restroom.

I decided that I would call 911.

But Jahvon made a horrible discovery before I could make that call.

Out of the restroom came Jahvon, carrying a lifeless but familiar figure in his powerful arms. He walked toward us with tears coming down his face like a river. Jahvon was carrying Mr. Ferrante. Our adopted uncle. The man who had taken us in when my dad was desperate and needed a job and a place to stay. A man who had always been good to our family. A man who always greeted us with a smile and a kind word.

I put my hand gently on his head and said in a painful whisper, "No." We were all crying.

Joshua said in a pained voice, "I could not find Daddy anywhere."

Jahvon lowered Mr. Ferrante's body to the ground. Still holding his head in his right hand, Jahvon went down on one knee.

Then, with a sobbing voice, Joshua asked a question that I had no answer to. "Who would do this? Why would anyone want to hurt innocent people like Mr. Ferrante? *Why?*" Then Joshua said, "And where is Daddy?"

I had no answer. At least not until I found a device that had been left at the front desk. It was a black piece of technology that looked like a sophisticated radio. Attached to the device was a message written on a piece of paper. The message read, "Prodigies, turn on by pressing the green button."

We knew that this had to be for us. Who else could be called a prodigy? Who could it be that could possibly refer to us as prodigies?

Jahvon pressed the button. It was clear in our minds that whoever was asking us to press this button was also responsible for this massacre. We did not know if it was a bomb. But we had to press it; we had to find a clue to where our father was.

We agreed that Jahvon would press the button. If it was a bomb, he could survive it.

Jahvon pressed the button while Joshua and I stayed in the kitchen. But there was no explosion.

Joshua and I returned to Jahvon and the device at the front desk.

To our surprise, a holographic image hovered in the air about six feet above the device. I studied it closely. It was a sophisticated form of communication, something like Skype but much more advanced.

The holograph showed four individuals. Three were looking back at us. We could see that the individuals were in a room with no furniture. They all were armed men with black camouflage uniforms. One of the men appeared very muscular and had a bald head. The man who had his back to us. It was this man who spoke, even as he faced the other direction.

Even though my brothers and I had superpowers, and these unknown individuals were in a different location from us, we felt fear. We felt fear because in our hearts we knew we were facing pure evil.

"Well, well, well. My dear little prodigies have grown up so much. I am so very proud of you. After all…" The man with his back to us laughed. "I…am…your…creator."

My brothers and I gasped. When the man said that he was our "creator," we knew who he was. This was who had done all those bad things that Daddy had told us about. This was the one that Daddy tried all those years to keep us from. This was the notorious Nicholas Hammerstein, known in the intelligence community as the Creator. That meant that the big bald guy next to him had to be his right-hand man, Ajax.

Hammerstein turned around, and we saw his face. "I know you boys have a lot of questions. Well, let me start giving you some answers. I was able to find you because your good deed at the bank was caught on camera and played before the whole world. As I am sure your daddy told you, there are a lot of cameras downtown. The Dawn of Shadow has eyes everywhere. Once word got out that thirty dangerous terrorists were taken down by a bunch of kids, well..." Hammerstein laughed. "I knew that had to be my little prodigies. I then hacked into all the security cameras in the area, including the ones in the sewers. I was able to determine your location by just looking at all the cameras in the area. Traffic light cameras, security cameras. You see, cameras can be remotely hacked and all the data downloaded to another location. Finding you was just a matter of time. I just followed the trail. Your activity at the bank was the starting place. Then I found out where you lived, and I had my men surround the location. Your father was smart. He knew it would only be a matter of time before I found you. That was probably why he had you start packing, so you could leave in a hurry. Only by then it was too late. I put your building under surveillance. I just needed to wait for him to get away from you. That is when my men quietly closed down Ferrante's and snatched your daddy. They made sure to do things quiet, while you watched television. After all, I would not have wanted you to do to my men what you did to those terrorists at the bank." Hammerstein laughed. "Oh, by the way, I want to thank you. I want to thank you for taking out those terrorists at the bank. You see, we at the Dawn of the Shadow establish a lot of relationships with terrorists all over the world. They do killings for us, and in return we either pay them with money or with some of our weapons and technology. The ones you took down at the bank were a small group that did some work for the Dawn of the Shadow in the past. We gave them some of our technology. I am sure you remember the energy field that they used to protect their bomb. That was a gift from us. But you, my little prodigies, you figured out how to deactivate the field. And you defeated all thirty men in combat. Armed men. Very good."

Then Jahvon interrupted in anger. He yelled the question that we all had: "Why did you kill these people, and where is our daddy?"

Joshua yelled, "Yeah, where is he?"

Hammerstein laughed at their outburst. "Ajax, bring their father into view." The big bald guy who we now knew was Ajax smiled and walked out of the holographic image. In two seconds, he returned, dragging our father, chained and gagged.

My brothers and I gasped at what we saw.

Hammerstein said, "As you can see, your daddy is alive and with me. Years ago your father took something very precious from me. He took you three. I promised him that I would make him pay a terrible price for what he did. I wanted to hurt those around him. That is why I had my men kill everyone in the restaurant."

Ajax then said, "It was my pleasure to kill that fat Italian owner of the restaurant. I strangled the life out of him with my bare hands." He threw back his head and laughed.

Jahvon's fists clenched as Ajax bragged about killing someone we cared about.

Hammerstein continued, "You are probably wondering what happens next. Tell me, my little prodigy..." He pointed through the screen at me.

Hammerstein was aware perhaps by watching the video footage of us in the bank that I was the one with the highly developed mind. He was right. He and I were about to engage in a back-and-forth dialogue. Like a law student and law professor exercising the Socratic method.

"Tell me, have you ever heard of Dr. Ramesh Patel?" Hammerstein asked.

I responded, "Uh, yes."

Hammerstein, smiling, then asked a question to which he already knew the answer. "Who is he?"

I answered, "Dr. Patel is a brilliant billionaire scientist and philanthropist. He is a graduate of Stanford. He earned his wealth from his company, Solarworld, Inc. He has created and sold the most effective and efficient solar panels in the world. In fact, thanks to his partnership with NASA, he was able to develop five powerful satellites that are now hovering in earth's orbit in space."

Hammerstein's eyes widened as I spoke. He gleefully said, "Yes, continue, my little prodigy, continue."

I continued, "The satellites are in space because they have special technology built into each one. Each satellite has the most sophisticated solar panels ever created. The panels will be able to absorb vast amounts of solar energy. This energy will be projected by the satellites to specific targets on earth's surface. There the energy will be absorbed and most importantly stored for the use of mankind. The hope of Dr. Patel is that he will be able to store and channel enough energy to power all of man's needs. It has always been Dr. Patel's vision that man would one day no longer need energy from sources such as oil and nuclear power. Instead, man will rely on the greatest energy source there is: the sun.

"Dr. Patel is perhaps the greatest environmentalist that ever lived. His whole life is dedicated to producing alternative energy for the benefit of mankind. Dr. Patel is a good man. He would never work for an evil organization like the Dawn of the Shadow."

Hammerstein laughed. Then he took a breath and enthusiastically said, "You are right, my little prodigy. He would never knowingly work for us. Everything you said about Patel and his technology and his vision is all *true*. We at the Dawn of the Shadow have had our eyes on him for years. We have been with him all of his professional life. Our people have infiltrated his company, Solarworld. Underneath Dr. Patel's nose we made some slight...adjustments to his technology. Yes, his five solar-paneled satellites absorb a tremendous amount of solar energy from the sun. However, we at the Dawn of the Shadow have adjusted the technology so that the energy is not conveyed to earth and stored; instead, the satellites have been weaponized. Now the energy that will come down to the earth will be energy that cannot be stored. It will be energy of destruction. The energy stored in the satellites will be amplified one hundred times. Once amplified, it will rain down fire upon the earth. That will bring the world to its knees."

I gasped. "If what you're saying is true, then millions of people will die." I hoped that what Hammerstein said was not true.

"No, my little prodigy. Not millions. *Hundreds* of millions." Hammerstein laughed. "This will be from the first four satellites. These are the satellites that will do the most damage. The fifth one, although powerful, is not as powerful as the first four. However, it moves more readily in space than the first four. The fifth will halt any attack on us from any military force as we charge up the first four with enough energy to incinerate whole continents."

"But why would you do this?" I asked desperately.

"Because, my little prodigy, we are the Dawn of the Shadow. We have been at war with those who try to stop us for hundreds of years. Now, in forty-eight hours, the war will come to an end. We will destroy the United States, one state at a time. After we bring the mighty America to its knees, then China, Russia, and all of Europe will follow. The rest of the world will then bend its knee and bow to the High Masters and the Dawn of the Shadow. Our rule of this world will be complete. This remaking of the world will begin in forty-eight hours. And nothing and no one will be able to stop me. Not even freaks of nature like you.

"Now, you will no doubt try to stop me and rescue your precious father. I am telling you this because I want you to try. I am your maker. What I can make, I can destroy. Your father and I will be waiting for you at the facility from which I will remake the world. There I will kill his whole family. I really don't want to kill you. After all, I made you. However, the High Masters have concluded, and I agree, that so long as you are alive you are a threat to the Dawn of the Shadow. Therefore, you have to die. But first I want you to see something. Ajax!"

Ajax stepped forth upon Hammerstein's command. He ordered the two other men to hold our father still. Then Ajax put his face right next to my father's face. My brothers and I were very fearful as to what would happen next. We were equally frustrated that, whatever was about to happened, we were powerless to stop it.

Ajax then said to my dad in a British accent, "Hey, Jordan, like old times, eh?" Ajax was referring to the time that he beat my father to a pulp while he was chained to a wall in North Carolina twelve years ago. Then Ajax began striking our father over and over again. Punches to the face. Punches to the body. My brothers and I screamed. We begged them to stop beating our father. After three minutes of what seemed to be an endless amount of blows, Ajax finally stopped. Our father was so badly damaged from the onslaught that his head hung and blood dripped from his face.

Hammerstein, smiling, said, "I made your father a promise that he was going to pay for taking you from me. I am keeping my promise. I will kill your father. I will kill all of you. But first I am going to make sure that you all suffer." Then Hammerstein looked at us with a mock sad look and said in a soft tone, "It is really very sad. You three prodigies were once my greatest creation. I kidnapped and tortured all those genetic scientists all over the world to gain the knowledge to create you. I killed hundreds of men in an effort to create you. All my efforts now wasted, thanks to your father. It's *so* sad. You three should have been by my side. We would have conquered the world together. Yes, you three were my greatest creations." Hammerstein viciously grabbed our father by the chin and shook his face. "Now, thanks to your father, you have become my greatest failures." He took a deep breath and concluded, "Good-bye, my little prodigies. I know your going to try and rescue your dad. I will be waiting for you at Solarworld's headquarters in Washington. When we meet again, you will die." Then the feed switched off, and the holographic image of Hammerstein, his men, and our father disappeared.

Joshua and Jahvon began yelling, "Wait, wait, Daddy...Daddy!"

The tears flowed from our eyes down our faces. Our world had just been turned upside down. Hours ago we were on top of the mountain, feeling great about saving people at the bank. Now we were at the bottom of the valley, feeling worse than we had ever felt and surrounded by the dead bodies of the workers in the restaurant. Finding dead a man we cared about. Seeing our father beaten and in the hands of an evil man. Joshua and Jahvon were confused and frustrated. Each rambling as to what we should do. Neither thinking straight due to this emotional moment.

Finally I yelled at the top of my lungs: *"Quiet!"*

I told my brothers we had to calm down and come up with a plan. I reminded them that this situation was bigger than us.

Despite our pain, we had to focus. Hammerstein was going to kill millions. If what he said about the technology of Solarworld was true, then he had to be stopped. I convinced my brothers that we had to leave this place that we had called home for twelve years. We had to go to Washington to stop this madman.

We gathered our things, including Daddy's trunk. I called 911 to let them know about the people who'd been killed at the restaurant. We did not want to leave Mr. Ferrante. We wanted to continue to hold him and comfort his deceased body. But we knew we had to go. We each said good-bye to Mr. Ferrante and hugged his body before we left the building once and for all. We took whatever cash we could find in the restaurant. We were able to find $3,000. We needed all the money we could get for food and gas for the trip to Washington. We also packed as much food from the kitchen as we could. We took Mr. Ferrante's Ford SUV. Then, once we had everything we needed to travel, we left. With tears still coming down our cheeks and heavy hearts, we hit the road.

I did all the driving. I had to attach sticks to my legs because my legs were too short to reach the gas pedal and the brake.

We had superpowers, but we were traumatized by what had just happened. As I drove, we were all quiet. We all wanted revenge against Hammerstein and Ajax for what they had done to our daddy, Mr. Ferrante, and the others.

Chapter 13

Evil Plans Put into Action

Hammerstein, Ajax, my father, and soldiers of the Dawn of the Shadow arrived by helicopter at the headquarters of Solarworld. Solarworld was a five-story facility of more than thirty thousand square feet. But two main chambers mattered most to Hammerstein: the communications chamber and the chamber that held the main computer. Hammerstein wanted to be able to communicate with the US government as he launched his evil plan upon the world. He and his men were able to take control of the satellites and operate them from the communications chamber.

My father, dragged in chains though the facility, saw dead bodies and blood everywhere. Before his arrival, Hammerstein had ordered his agents who had already infiltrated Solarworld to begin the operation. These people were just posing as workers for the company. In reality they were soldiers of the Dawn of the Shadow. Upon Hammerstein's command, they murdered all the workers who were not part of the Dawn of the Shadow. It was a bloodbath. Good, hard-working young men and women who were dedicated to fighting climate change had their throats cut or were shot in the head by someone they had thought was just a coworker. Sixty people were reduced to thirty—the half who did not work for the Dawn of the Shadow killed by the half who did.

Hammerstein and his men, however, intended to kill more than thirty people. They intended to kill millions.

Ajax and two other men put my father in a painfully familiar position against the wall in the computer chamber. They chained him up in a crucifix position. Just as they had done years ago in North Carolina. Hammerstein then placed a very sophisticated-looking video camera eight feet away, facing my father. My father was curious as to why Hammerstein would record him being tortured and held captive.

Hammerstein walked up to my father and said in a sarcastic tone, "Jordan, I hope you like your position. I just wanted you to feel at home for old time's sake." Hammerstein and Ajax laughed, and Hammerstein continued, "Trust me, Jordan, I have made sure that you won't be able to break out of these chains. There is no weak wall holding the chains this time. I am sure you are wondering what the camera is for. Don't worry, you will soon find out."

Hammerstein's men set up holographic images in the communication chamber. The images were live video feeds of the five satellites.

Then Hammerstein yelled out a command: "Initiate the reshaping of the world!"

Hammerstein's men at the control panels pressed buttons and pulled levers.

At that moment, the fifth of the five satellites began to move in space. It positioned itself over Washington, DC. Then, with unbelievable energy, it projected a powerful solar blast down upon the earth. The blast was a quarter of the size of a football field. It destroyed several buildings, killing dozens of people. Then the satellite moved again; it fired upon another target, and then another. People died in high numbers from the power of the blast. There was incredible destruction. Buildings were destroyed and people were incinerated.

The US government mobilized its armed forces. The president was taken to a secure and hidden location. His national security team was convened. The president and his team desperately sought answers as to what was going on and how to stop the satellite.

They were able to determine that the fifth satellite was being operated from a communication signal coming from the headquarters of Solarworld. The government deployed drones and fighter jets to destroy that facility, hoping to stop any more communications to the fifth satellite.

Unfortunately, Hammerstein was prepared. He had the satellite defend that location. Any drone hellfire missile or fighter jet that came anywhere near the facility was blown out of the sky by the fifth satellite. The precision, speed, and accuracy of the fifth satellite was incredible.

Dr. Patel, the billionaire founder of Solarworld, was giving a lecture at Stanford University in California while the destruction was going on in Washington. Secret

Service entered the large auditorium and swiftly took him away. The crowd and Dr. Patel were in shock as to what was going on.

The Secret Service took Dr. Patel to a secure facility. There a video communication link connected him with the president of the United States and his national security team.

The president demanded answers as to what was going on at his facility. Dr. Patel was just as surprised as anyone. He did confirm that the satellite causing the destruction was his, but he did not understand why his technology was operating this way.

The CIA had received an anonymous communication that warned of an imminent terror threat against United States greater than 9/11. The CIA sent the video directly to President Jamison's location. Once the video played, it became clear what the United States and the world were facing. It was an attack by an old enemy, one who Western governments had been fighting for years. It was a message from the Dawn of the Shadow.

On the video was a message directly to the president from Hammerstein himself. In the video Hammerstein said, "Greetings, President Jamison. I wanted you to know what was going on. After all, there is nothing that you can do to stop what will happen. The war between the world and the Dawn of the Shadow is about to come to an end. By now your intelligence and military apparatus has informed you that the destruction that has been inflicted on Washington so far has come from one of the five satellites of Solarworld. The other four are the more powerful satellites. They even now are charging up and absorbing vast amounts of energy from the sun. Once those four satellites are fully charged, their energy shall be amplified a thousand fold. The satellites will then blast down upon the earth with enough destructive power to destroy all of Washington and parts of Maryland and Virginia. With the exception of this facility, of course. Then I will direct the four satellites to concentrate their power on every state in the union. Millions will die. I will bring this country to its knees. Even if you could destroy the Solarworld facility, you would not stop the four satellites from blasting down on Washington and killing millions. Once the process has begun, it can only be stopped by commands given from this facility.

"I know you are going to try to stop me. That is why I have the fifth satellite. It will stop any aggression you take against the headquarters in Washington. There is nothing you can do, Mr. President. As I said, the war is going to end. The world will run according to the dictates of the Dawn of the Shadow. The only real purpose of this message is to let you and the rest of the world know who it was that brought the United States of America to its knees. Oh, I almost forgot. Be sure to let Dr. Patel know that all his staff who were not part of the Dawn of the Shadow are now dead. Their services were no longer needed. Thank him also for providing us this wonderful technology. I will be sure to make good use of it." The video ended with Hammerstein laughing.

Hammerstein was recognized as being a major player in the terrorist group Dawn of the Shadow. The communication was networked to Dr. Patel's location in California. The president and his staff wanted him to hear what Hammerstein said so Patel could tell them how to stop this monster.

Dr. Patel had seen the entire message from Hammerstein. The scientist was in shock and heartbroken that all of his staff at the facility were now dead. Many had been his friends. He was also heartbroken that the technology that he had spent a lifetime developing for good had been corrupted by a terrorist organization for evil. Dr. Patel was emotionally hurt by the video of Hammerstein and what he was told in his debriefing by the Secret Service. He put his head down and cried.

Under his breath, Dr. Patel murmured an emotional, "Dear God, no. My friends, dead. All my work, my vision corrupted. My God."

Through the video feed, President Jamison saw Dr. Patel's emotional anguish.

In an angry and frustrated voice, the president yelled at Dr. Patel, "Dammit, man, pull yourself together! This is not the time to give in to sorrow. People are dying and more people are going to die unless we stop this madman. Now, you know this facility and the technology better than anyone. You have got to help us find a way to stop this monster."

Dr. Patel heard the president's words. He took a deep breath and said, "Yes, Mr. President. I'll do what I can." Dr. Patel always carried his own equipment with him to monitor his technology. He took out his briefcase. It held a monitoring device that was networked into his company. From it Dr. Patel was able to determine that what Hammerstein had said was true.

Dr. Patel then said to the president and the national security team, "I have confirmed, based on my readings of what is happening with the satellites, that what that madman said was true. According to my calculations, it will take ninety minutes from now for the four satellites to charge up before they can send a blast of destructive solar energy down upon the earth."

The president then asked Dr. Patel the question that was on everyone's mind. "How do we stop the satellites from charging up?"

Dr. Patel answered, "Even if you destroy the facility, it will not stop the satellites from absorbing the sun's energy and directing it down upon the earth. The only way to stop them is by activating the main computer's self-destruct command for the satellites, which can only be done from the main computer chamber within the facility. But if this madman is as smart as I think he is, then he would have found a way of deactivating the self-destruct mechanism. At least he would have found a way of deactivating the computer's ability to trigger the self-destruct mechanism. If he did this, then the self-destruct mechanism can only be activated by someone sitting in the chair of that chamber and manually doing all the very complex mathematical formulas within three seconds per question. But no one on the planet can perform such mathematical calculations at such speed."

General Madson, who was one of the Joint Chiefs of Staff, interjected, "If what the doctor is saying is correct, then we have to get a team in the facility to make sure that self-destruct mechanism is activated. Assuming that Hammerstein has not shut off the computer's ability to trigger the self-destruct."

The president then responded to the general with another obvious question. "How are we going to get our military personnel past that fifth satellite? It's incinerating anything that comes near the facility."

The general said, "With a diversion, sir. We send in a lot of firepower from the west of the facility. Hammerstein will be forced to focus the fifth satellite on what's coming at him from the west. At the same time we have a platoon of marines and a unit of Navy SEALs enter the facility from the east. By the time our military personnel get within a certain proximity of the facility, they will be safe. Hammerstein won't risk using the fifth satellite's firepower because our troops will be too close to the facility."

"Sounds good," responded the president. "Does anyone know how close our people have to get before Hammerstein decides not to risk the facility being hit by the fifth satellite?"

"Fifty yards, Mr. President. Fifty yards. That's how close they need to get," Dr. Patel abruptly blurted out.

The president asked Dr. Patel, "Are you sure?"

Dr. Patel nodded his head confidently and said, "Yes, I am. Hammerstein may have modified the power of the sun's rays but nothing else. Our design was to always keep the fifth satellite from coming down on our facility. This was to always make sure that the satellite's rays do not interfere with any of our other technology at the facility."

The general then stated, "With the fifth satellite having such destructive power, it's likely that Hammerstein did not make any adjustments in that regard. In his arrogance, he probably does not think we would launch a ground assault against him."

The president then said, "Get a force on the ground and get a force in the air attacking from the west. I want every drone and fighter jet we can muster in the air at the location ASAP."

The general stated, "We already have a platoon of marines and SEALs at the target location, sir. The command will be given as soon as the hellfire missiles start firing upon the facility. We have to have some contingency in the event that the computer's self-destruct has been deactivated."

Dr. Patel said, "Other than someone activating the self-destruct manually, there is no other contingency. There are pylons that if activated can project an energy field to prevent the solar energy from coming down from the satellites. However, this shield is only temporary. It would probably buy whoever or whatever is doing the self-destruct sequence an extra fifteen minutes of time."

The general asked, "Where would the pylons need to be activated, Doctor?"

"Based on my readings of where the four satellites are pointing, the pylons would have to be taken to the Washington Monument and activated there. There the pylons would be able generate a shield in the atmosphere wide enough to temporarily block the blasts from the satellites. The pylons are located at the facility itself," responded the doctor.

The president ordered that all traffic be stopped from the facility to the Washington Monument. If necessary, they would be able to get the pylons there as fast as possible. Transport would have to be on the ground, since the fifth satellite was blowing things out of the sky.

The president, nervous and frustrated that the country was under attack during his presidency, said in a voice that had both anger and fear, "All right, people, let's do it. Get our teams in the facility. Get to that computer chamber and get those pylons where they need to go to stop this devil Hammerstein."

The US government devised a plan, and they began the process of executing that plan. What no one there knew at that time was they were going to need the help of three very special twelve-year-olds.

***

While the US government was responding to Hammerstein's actions against humanity, my brothers and I were driving into Washington. The radio was filled with news accounts of the destruction. We had been driving to Washington from New York for about six hours. I had to make stops to get some rest. I could drive, but I was no truck driver. We could see the blast come down from the sky in the distance.

When I saw it, I said, "It's started."

There was a mass panic in the streets. People were desperately trying to get out of the city. We knew that there was no way for us to get to the facility in time by car. We needed to find another way. Just then I could see helicopters flying above. Some were law enforcement and others were media helicopters.

I used the SUV's GPS to find the closest helicopter hangar in the area. I was able to find one that was about five miles from our location. Luckily we had somewhat of an advantage. People were trying to leave the area we were trying to get to. So we were going in the opposite direction of most traffic. But it was still difficult traveling.

Finally, after about forty-five minutes, we made it to an aviation facility. This is where many of the news stations had their helicopters. We parked the car about a half-mile from the entrance. Then we went on foot. I made sure to park the car someplace safe and secure. We had all of our belongings in it, and I did not want it to get ticketed or towed. We put on our little makeshift masks and started on foot toward the front gate of the hangar.

Guards stood at the gate. We did not want to beat them up for just doing their jobs. But millions of lives were at stake, and time was not on our side. We came in fast and hard. Joshua ran up to the guards and kicked them in the knees. This caused them to fall to the ground. Once they were on the ground, Joshua quickly gave them karate chops in the back of the head, knocking them out. Jahvon then grabbed me and, with his powerful legs, jumped over the thirty-foot gate. That was one thrill ride to be flying over a gate in your brother's arms. Joshua ran up and over the gate with his superspeed and agility.

Once we were on the other side, we ran to a hangar about thirty yards away. But we had been spotted. Security had seen Joshua on camera beating up the guards at the gate. Now more security personnel came toward us.

Jahvon said to Joshua and me, "Go get us a chopper, and I will stop them."

Once we got to the hangar area, we saw several helicopters and some small planes. I told Joshua to find a chopper with a pilot; we could not risk having no keys. Joshua with his super-speed ran ahead of me. He reached a chopper with a pilot inside and kicked the pilot in the face. Then he picked up a toolbox that was on the chopper and hit the pilot on the back of the head. The pilot was knocked out.

I ran to the chopper. Joshua had taken the keys, and he gave them to me. I was breathing heavily after all the running. Plus all the adrenaline that was pumping in me. Joshua was breathing even harder than I was.

Here my brothers and I were trying to save the world, and we were committing the crimes of breaking and entering and assault. The irony was incredible to me.

After I spent thirty seconds fumbling with the keys, I finally got the right one for the helicopter. I told Joshua to put the headphones on so we could communicate when the chopper was in the air.

Joshua asked me, "Are you sure you can fly this thing?"

I said with the utmost confidence, "I can fly anything." I started the engine. Everything looked good, and there was plenty of fuel.

More security personnel drove toward us, their sirens blaring. Jahvon was still on the ground, while I was trying to get in the air. We needed more time. The guards, thinking that Jahvon was just a regular kid, tried to swerve around him. Jahvon jumped in the air and landed on top of the vehicle's engine. But he landed with such force that he caused the vehicle to flip over, and the car ended up on its back. The security guards were stunned and disoriented by what had just happened. Jahvon flipped the car back to its proper side to keep the two security personnel from being trapped upside down. His actions gave me enough time to get the chopper in the air.

I flew to where Jahvon was and hovered twenty-five feet above him. That was within his vertical jumping range. Jahvon bent his legs and squatted down and quickly exploded upward with a powerful jump. He jumped high enough to grab the side of the chopper, and his weight caused the chopper to dip momentarily as he climbed inside.

Joshua gave him some earphones, and Jahvon asked me a question that was familiar. "Hey, Jason, you sure you can fly this thing?"

Joshua answered for me: "He can fly anything."

I had the location of the facility memorized. I knew the coordinates from looking it up online and from the SUV's GPS. So I knew where to fly the chopper. I told my brothers, "Hold on. Next stop, save the world."

Jahvon said, "Let's do it."

Joshua said, "Let's go get 'em." We were all nervous but determined to take on our maker and beat him. Regardless of the cost.

Chapter 14

The Alliance

The US government launched their attack on Hammerstein and the facility. They positioned a platoon of forty marines and ten Navy SEALs on the ground. These two teams were assigned to enter the facility and activate the computer's self-destruct mechanism. At the same time, they were to get the pylons to the Washington Monument, where they could be activated to help buy millions of people more time. The men were all dedicated soldiers, and their hearts were pumping. They knew they would only have small window of time to storm the facility before the fifth satellite targeted them. No one knew what was waiting for them at the facility. Hammerstein was very smart and very dangerous. All the soldiers felt that a villain like Hammerstein would expect a ground assault. They had to be prepared for anything. In the meantime, they waited for the air strike.

As planned, dozens of drones fired hellfire missiles at the facility, along with missiles from fighter jets. As expected, Hammerstein had the fifth satellite destroy everything that came at the facility by air. The sky lit up with an unbelievable amount of explosions. Not to mention the brilliance of the fifth satellite blasting concentrated solar energy upon the earth.

Hammerstein was able to see what was going from cameras on the satellites. He and Ajax saw the ground forces coming from the east as the air attack came from the west.

Ajax laughed and said, "You were right. These fools would try to attack us on both fronts. From the air and on the ground. They knew we would not ignore the air strike. Now watch their forces come at us from the east on the ground."

Hammerstein watched the Navy SEALs and the marines sprinting toward the facility. He said to Ajax, "Take our men to give these soldiers a warm greeting on the grounds of the facility. Also send another team to kill off any undesirables that try to get in from the roof."

Ajax responded with a firm and gleeful, "My pleasure."

Ajax left, giving orders on a communication device for a team to go with him to the grounds on the facility's eastern side. He ordered another team of the Dawn of the Shadow to be prepared for invaders on the roof. Ajax was almost as much of a natural leader as Hammerstein.

Hammerstein turned to my father, still chained to the wall, battered and beaten, and said, "It looks like your military brothers are coming in for the rescue. Watch, Jordan, what is happening on the screens. Watch as your military kin die." My father felt sad for those soldiers. He knew they were headed for a trap. Similar to how Hammerstein had trapped his unit over twelve years ago in Syria. Then my father's thoughts fell upon his greatest treasure, his sons. *Where are they? Are they safe?* These were the thoughts that were running through his mind at that moment.

Ajax and his team set up tactical positions on the roof and the grounds of the facility.

The Navy SEALs came into the building at entirely separate location. They quickly launched grapples onto the rooftops. With the utmost speed and stealth, the SEALs scaled the one-hundred-foot wall to the roof. Once on the wall, they would use an electronic map to find their way to where the computer chamber was. At the same time, the marines stormed toward the main entrance on the west side of the facility.

As the marines were coming, Ajax commanded, "Kill the infidels."

His men fired upon the marines. The marines fired back. On the roof Ajax's men knew exactly where the SEALs were, due to the cameras throughout the facility. They began firing upon the SEALs. The SEALs took defensive positions and returned fire on the soldiers of the Dawn of the Shadow. It was an incredible gun battle. At first the SEALs and the marines were holding their own with the Dawn of the Shadow. But time was on the side of the Dawn of the Shadow. Hammerstein and Ajax did not need to kill off all the marines and SEALs. All they needed to do was make sure that nothing interfered with the four charging satellites. So a stalemate was still a win at this moment for the Dawn of the Shadow.

Bullets flew everywhere. Grenades were thrown. One marine even took out a rocket launcher. The rocket launcher was fired at the soldiers of the Dawn of the Shadow, killing some of them. However, the Dawn of the Shadow had explosive rockets themselves, which they used to kill some marines. The SEALs were phenomenal marksmen, but they could not advance. The soldiers of the Dawn of the Shadow were positioned behind structures on the roof that provided cover; they could not be hit by the SEALs' firepower.

President Jamison, General Madson, and the rest of the national security team were watching. As was Hammerstein. Hammerstein watched and laughed, while the president and his generals watched with despair. Time was running out. Only about forty minutes remained before the satellites directed their energy upon the earth. It seemed like things were hopeless.

President Jamison yelled, "Dammit, isn't there anything we can do to get our men in there faster?"

General Madson, in a frustrated tone, said, "No, sir, the firepower from the enemy is more than sufficient to keep our forces at bay with that limited ground force."

By this time the airstrikes on the facility had stopped. The fifth satellite had destroyed all the air missiles and now focused on the ground forces. The ground forces that were engaged in combat with the soldiers of the Dawn of the Shadow were safe from being incinerated by the fifth satellite. They were inside the fifty-yard radius within which the fifth satellite would not fire. However, no more ground troops were able to enter.

Then things grew worse for the troops on the ground. From behind the soldiers of the Dawn of the Shadow appeared red glowing eyes. The eyes belonged to figures that stepped out of the shadows. They were the high guard of the Dawn of the Shadow known as the Blade of the Shadow. The deadly killer robots. They were dressed in all-black garb. They looked similar to Japanese ninjas except for the red eyes. Five of them ran toward the marines. The marines fired upon them. The bullets just bounced off them, having no effect. The Blade of the Shadow took out pistols of their own. They began firing upon the marines. Now the marines were taking fire from the soldiers of the Dawn of the Shadow plus the Blade of the Shadow. The screams of marines hit by enemy bullets echoed throughout the courtyard. The marines could not fall back too far or they would be back within the range of the fifth satellite. But the Blade of the Shadow began to close in on them. The frustration of the president and his generals mounted as they saw their soldiers die.

Then one of the generals said, "We have an incoming aircraft, sir, heading toward the facility."

The president and his generals were shocked.

"Is it one of our military aircraft?" the president said.

The general said, "No, sir. It appears to be commercial. In fact, based on the satellite feed we are getting, it's a news helicopter."

The president, shocked and frustrated that things seemed to be getting worse, yelled, "What? Who is foolish enough to be flying that helicopter near that facility? They are going to be incinerated out of the sky. Try to raise whoever is flying that thing and tell them to steer the hell away from that area."

One of his staff nervously and hesitantly said, "Sir, that has already been done. The pilot of the helicopter is requesting to speak to you. It's...uh...um, well...uh...um, sir..."

The president, frustrated by this staffer, yelled, "Well, spit it out. Who is the pilot of that helicopter?"

The staffer said, "Sir, it's, um, a twelve-year-old kid who says that he and his brothers can help the soldiers and, um...uh, and I quote, 'beat up the bad guys.'"

The president said to the general, "Millions of people are only thirty minutes or so away from getting incinerated and some punk kids decided to steal and go joyriding in a news helicopter. This has got to be a joke!"

Hammerstein also saw the helicopter. One of his men asked Hammerstein if he should have the satellite incinerate the helicopter. Hammerstein joyfully said, "No. I like the idea of this being on television so up close. The world can now get a better view of the Dawn of the Shadow taking over the world. Let them in and roll their cameras."

The helicopter that everyone was talking about was my brothers and me. I informed my brothers that the president of the United States did not want to talk to me. Then I told my brothers that I believed we wouldn't get blown out of the sky because Hammerstein would see that this was not a military aircraft. I had a hunch that Hammerstein's ego was as big as his evil. So I figured he would love to have as much of an audience as possible. I was right. Thinking that we were really a news chopper, Hammerstein let us pass the fifty-yard mark and did not incinerate us out of the sky.

As we flew closer to the facility, we could see the intense firefight on the ground. We could see that the military could not advance on either the roof or the ground, and the scary things with red eyes were killing the marines on the ground with their firepower.

I was flying the chopper about seven thousand feet in the air. Everyone on the ground could see us. However, that did not stop the gun battle.

I said to Jahvon and Joshua, "It looks like the military is trying to get into the facility. The Dawn of the Shadow are holding them at bay. We have got to help the military."

Jahvon said in an excited voice, "Fly me over the fighting on the ground right in the middle by those pillars. I'll just drop in."

Joshua then said, "Fly low to the roof behind the bad guys."

I flew the chopper above the battleground between the Dawn of the Shadow and the marines. I hovered in between the Blade of the Shadow and the marines. Jahvon was excited about joining the fight. In his excitement, he began shaking the whole helicopter.

I yelled at Jahvon, "Stop jumping up and down. You're going to cause the chopper to fall apart." Jahvon struggled to control his excitement and fear and stopped himself from shaking apart the helicopter with his superstrength.

Joshua said to Jahvon, "You ready, brother?"

Jahvon said in an excited and confident manner, "Yes."

Jahvon then took a deep breath, stood at the edge of the opening on the chopper, and yelled, "Look out below."

Jahvon hopped out of the helicopter while I was hovering it seven thousand feet in the air. Everyone was in shock. The president and his men, Hammerstein, the marines, and the soldiers of the Dawn of the Shadow saw a kid jump out of a helicopter. Everyone was about to find out that this was no suicide attempt. As Jahvon was falling at great speed to the ground, Hammerstein's heart jumped as he recognized who he was looking at. It was one of his creations. My father was also watching the screen. My father's heart leapt because he was looking at one of his sons.

Jahvon slammed to the ground with a thunderous *boom*. His density, combined with the speed with which he fell, left a hole in the ground that was about five feet wide and three feet deep. Jahvon jumped out of the hole. The marines paused. They paused because they were in shock to see a kid survive a fall from such a height and then just jump out of the hole that his fall had created.

While the marines momentarily stopped their shooting, the Blade of the Shadow and the soldiers for the Dawn of the Shadow did not. They continued to fire, now firing upon their new target, Jahvon. The bullets were bouncing off Jahvon like raindrops. Pinging sounds could be heard as bullets bounced off of Jahvon's body. All of this was being captured on film by the cameras in the area. Hammerstein and my father were able to see everything that was occurring on the facility grounds. At the same time, the president and the generals were able to see what was going on from their overhead satellites still under military control as well as from cams mounted on some of the marines.

Jahvon ran up to a pillar in the courtyard to the right of his position. He slammed his shoulder into the pillar much like a fullback would block a linebacker from tackling a half-back in football. Jahvon hit the pillar with such force that the fifteen-foot-tall, three-foot-wide marble pillar cracked at the point of impact. Then it began to fall toward Jahvon, who ran underneath the pillar and caught it.

General Madson said what everyone was thinking at that moment. "How is this possible?" That pillar had to weigh about four tons. It was now being held in the air by a kid.

Jahvon focused his attention on the five members of the Blade of the Shadow advancing on him. He took a step and, with a mighty push of his arms, flung the huge pillar at them. The pillar met its mark, destroying the inhuman agents of evil.

Jahvon then ran to the pillar and picked it up. He advanced upon the soldiers of the Dawn of the Shadow still firing from the ground entrance of the facility.

The general picked up a communication device and said to the marine commander on the ground, "That boy or whatever the hell he is has just given you an opening, soldier. Now make the most of it."

The marine commander on the ground needed that stern command to get him focused, not just on what he was seeing but on the opportunity that this mysterious, superstrong kid had just given the marines.

With the five killer robots destroyed and Jahvon now advancing with the pillar upon the entrance of the facility, the marines had the cover from enemy fire they needed to advance upon the facility.

The marine commander yelled at his men, "Get to the kid and return fire!"

Ten marines ran up to Jahvon, took cover behind the pillar that he was carrying, and began firing upon the Dawn of the Shadow soldiers. Jahvon allowed them to get close enough to shoot down those soldiers. The soldiers of the Dawn of the Shadow's bullets bounced off the huge marble pillar. At closer range now, the marines' bullets were hitting the mark. The marines could not believe what was going on. A kid was carrying a huge object that weighed tons and was giving them cover against firepower. The marine platoon commander fought back his disbelief and was making the most of the situation. This was evident when he made a request from Jahvon while he was carrying the pillar.

He said, "Hey, kid, move a little to the left."

Jahvon complied with the request and with his superstrength moved the pillar a little to the left as he was going forward. This allowed the marines to shoot down some more soldiers of the Dawn of the Shadow that they could not reach before due to their positions by the main entrance.

Meanwhile, up on the roof, the SEALs were in a fierce firefight with the soldiers of the Dawn of the Shadow.

Hammerstein, like everyone else, saw what Jahvon was doing. "So, my dear little prodigies have finally made it to the party." Then, issuing a command to the soldiers of the Dawn of the Shadow on the roof, he yelled, "Shoot down that helicopter!"

The Dawn of the Shadow on the roof refocused their firepower from the Navy SEALs to Joshua and me, still in the helicopter. The bullets came at us mercilessly. I tried desperately to move the chopper out of their line of fire.

"Hold on!" I yelled to Joshua.

Joshua was gripping the handles in the roof of the chopper. We could hear the *ping, ping, pow* sounds of bullets hitting the chopper.

In a frightful panic, Joshua yelled, "They are shooting at us! They are shooting at us!"

I yelled back in a frustrated tone at Joshua for telling me the obvious. "No kidding. You think?"

The bullets damaged the engine and the back propeller. We were spinning out of control. Fortunately, we were closer to the ground than we were than when Jahvon jumped out. The helicopter spun at incredible speed. I was feeling dizzy. Joshua did not mind the speed. He was able to make the world around him slow down in his mind because of his superspeed. He grabbed me and pulled me out of the pilot chair as we fell. When he saw the chopper go near two twenty-foot-high antennas on one of the rooftops, Joshua jumped out of the chopper while holding me with his right arm. With incredible speed and agility, he jumped onto the nearest of the two antennas. Sliding down it, he jumped to the next antenna while still holding on to me and then back again, moving from side to side, until finally we made it to the bottom. This put us on one of the rooftops of the huge facility behind where the SEALs were. The helicopter crashed to the ground at another part of the facility, making a huge explosion. I was dizzy and disoriented by what had just occurred. But Joshua wasn't. He told me to relax and that he was going to help the US military on the roof.

Then, with blinding speed, Joshua ran up to the position where the SEALs were. The firefight between them and the Dawn of the Shadow was continuing. One of the Navy SEALs looked at Joshua, surprised and shocked to see some kid seemingly appear out of nowhere. The SEAL said, "Stay down, kid, and where in the hell did you just come from?"

Joshua, breathing heavily from all of his athletic activity, said, "No time to explain. Just tell your men to not shoot me in the back and, oh, um, uh...I am going to need your gun. Thanks."

The SEAL, surprised by Joshua saying that he needed his gun, said, "Kid, you are not getting my gun. What the hell—"

With incredible speed, before the SEAL had time to react, Joshua took the sidearm out of his holster and ran toward the soldiers of the Dawn of the Shadow. Cameras were on the roof. Hammerstein and my dad could see all that was taking place from the communications chamber. Both men felt a sense of pride seeing what Joshua had done. One had pride in his son out of love. The other, pride in seeing his genius manifested. President Jamison, General Madson, and the other national security team could also see what was going on from the drone feed.

Joshua avoided the gunfire by running up and across the side of the wall. It looked as if magnetic boots allowed him to run sideways on the wall. But it was the momentum from his speed that allowed him to do this. Joshua ran over one hundred feet to where the Dawn of the Shadow were. He then ran behind the structures that gave the Dawn of the Shadow cover from the SEALs' firepower. Joshua had the added advantage that the soldiers of the Dawn of the Shadow were still in a firefight with the SEALs. So the enemy had to focus on the SEALs rather than Joshua, and he did not have to worry about having to dodge any bullets at that moment. Joshua took the firearm that he had taken from the Navy SEAL and gripped it by its barrel. Then one by one he hit the soldiers of the Dawn of the Shadow in the back of the head with the handle of the gun, knocking them out.

The SEAL commander, when he noticed that the enemy was not firing upon them anymore, said, "Hold your fire."

With guns drawn, the SEALs ran to the location where the Dawn of the Shadow had been firing upon them. The SEALs were shocked to see all ten hardcore killers knocked out and a skinny twelve-year-old boy standing victorious over them.

Joshua then handed the gun back to the SEAL he'd taken it from and said, "Thanks."

The SEAL, still shocked by what he'd just witnessed, said hesitantly, "Uh, you're welcome."

Back on the ground, the marines had killed all the soldiers of the Dawn of the Shadow, thanks to Jahvon using the huge pillar as a shield. Not needing the pillar anymore, Jahvon dropped it to the ground.

Over the next five minutes, my brothers and I regrouped with the military. The commanding military officers on the ground demanded to know who and what we were.

I said, "I know you must be linked up to the president of the United States, so I hope he listens to what I am going to say. We are on your side. Our actions just now should have proven that. We know that Hammerstein is in there, and we know what he is doing. The only way you are going stop those satellites is by helping me get to the computer chamber."

General Madson said to me via a communication device, "Kid, what are you?"

I took a deep breath and said the truth in one word, "Prodigy." Then I said, "I am sure you are monitoring the countdown before the four satellites destroy Washington. I know you have a lot of questions about us, but the most important thing right now is to stop this madman."

President Jamison introduced himself and said, "Kid, you're obviously very smart. You know that we need to get into the computer chamber and get the pylons to the Washington Monument."

I responded, "I do. But Hammerstein is too smart to have allowed the automatic computer sequence of the self-destruct to remain operational. I guarantee you that he disabled it. Which means that the self-destruct sequence can only be activated manually."

The president said, "Son, if your theory is true, then Hammerstein has already won. According to Dr. Patel, no human on earth can figure the mathematical formulas fast enough to activate the self-destruct mechanism."

I responded with a confident, "No one but me, Mr. President. No one but me."

The CIA director told the president and the generals what he'd heard about the Prodigy Project from intel chatter twelve years ago. Prodigies, he said, were to be used as weapons fighting on behalf of the Dawn of the Shadow. But these rumors had been dismissed when no evidence of the project coming to fruition ever surfaced.

The president then took a deep breath and said, "I know you just helped us fight off the soldiers of the Dawn of the Shadow. But I want you to give me another reason why we—why I—should trust you boys."

After a long pause I sadly said, "Simple, sir. That evil madman has our father, and we want him back."

The president then asked, "Who's your father, boy?"

"My father is Jordan Reyes," I responded.

Once I said my father's name, the intel people quickly pulled up his file. They saw that he was a war hero, a Navy SEAL. They saw how his unit had been found slaughtered. Categorized as missing in action, his body had never been recovered.

The president knew that time was running out. He could not believe what was happening, but he decided to take a chance with my brothers and me. There was no other option.

He said, "All right, let's give these boys whatever support they need. Let's get him to that computer chamber, and we need to get those pylons to the Washington Monument."

I smiled and said, "Thanks, Mr. President. My brother is best suited to get the pylons to the Washington Monument because of his speed. You are going to have to avoid the air because of the fifth satellite. Me and my other brother will go in and get my father. Then we will go to the computer chamber."

General Madson interrupted me by saying, "Negative, son. Time is wasting. If what you say is true, then we need you in the computer chamber as quickly as possible. You are going to need all the muscle you can get. So that strong brother of yours and the marine platoon will escort you to the chamber. As far as your other brother, I agree we will give him the pylons and have him run them to the Washington Monument."

Jahvon interrupted with the same question that Joshua and I had: "What about our father? We need to rescue him."

The general said in a sympathetic voice, "The SEALs will get your father, son."

I said, "I disagree. That monster is going to kill him. We have to rescue him." Then, from behind me, a firm but reassuring hand gripped my shoulder. It was one of the Navy SEALs. This was one tough and mean looking six-foot-one-inch man. Even in his uniform you could tell that he was in tip-top shape. He and the ten other SEALs stood around my brothers and me and looked at us with compassion.

One of the SEALs said, "Your father is one of us."

Another said, "We never met your dad, but he is our brother."

"We will get him out," another SEAL said. "You have our word."

That look in their eyes and their words convinced my brothers and me to trust them. Joshua, Jahvon, and I all looked at one another and slowly nodded our heads in agreement.

I then turned to the Navy SEAL who had referred to our father as a "brother" and said, "OK. Do you promise to get my daddy out?"

The SEAL looked my brothers and me in the eyes, nodded his head, and said, "Promise."

The decisions had been made in terms of our course of action. We were now in alliance with the US military. Jahvon and a platoon of marines were going to escort me to the computer chamber. Joshua was going to run the pylons to the Washington Monument. The SEALs were going to find a way into the communications chamber to rescue Daddy from Hammerstein. We knew that Hammerstein would try to keep my father with him. We also knew that Hammerstein was controlling the satellites from the communications chamber. So that had to be the location of my father as well.

The marines were able to recover the two small pylons from an area close to the entrance of the facility. They put the two pylons in a backpack that they then strapped around Joshua. It was like a green military school bag.

The SEALs fitted my brothers and me each with an earpiece. This was so command would be able to communicate with us. I gave Joshua my own device so that he could track me if he needed to. I only had one, so I gave it to Joshua since Jahvon was going to stay with me.

Meanwhile, Hammerstein was able to see but not hear the details of our meeting with the military. By this time Ajax had found his way back to the communications room. Hammerstein, Ajax, and their men had their own meeting to strategize a way to stop us from stopping them.

Hammerstein, watching us from one of the cameras on the facility, smiled. He smiled because he felt excited about taking on his own creations. He felt excited because in a matter of thirty minutes he was going to bring the United States and the world to its knees.

Hammerstein looked at my father in Ajax's presence and said, "Your sons are going to fail, Jordan. They are also going to join you today. In death." Then Hammerstein began to pace the communications room and gleefully said, "I know they are going to try to take the pylons to the Washington Monument." He turned to two of the Blade of the Shadow robots and said, "It was very kind of the High Masters to allow us to have some of the Blade of the Shadow to assist us today. Run the boy down and butcher him like a pig." He pointed to the image of Joshua on his screen to identify their target. Then Hammerstein turned to Ajax and said,

"Take the remaining Blade of the Shadow and kill that smart little prodigy. He will be protected by the marines and his strong brother. The marines will be easy to kill. As for that strong prodigy with the big afro, use the prototype weapon. His superstrength will be no match for it. Especially with you using it."

Ajax laughed and said, "Killing that strong kid will be fun." Then Ajax paused, and his smile went away. He looked at Hammerstein and said in a somber tone, "If there is anyone who could operate the computer, it's that damn smart prodigy. The one called Jason."

Hammerstein responded, "Indeed, he does have the intellect powerful enough to operate the computer. The only one on the planet who can. However, I am going to exploit a weakness that is pervasive in so many young people in the world today. That is…a lack of confidence." Hammerstein laughed.

Ajax joined his master in laughing. He then ordered two of the Blade of Shadow robots to go after Joshua. The other five he ordered to accompany him to kill the marines, me, and Jahvon.

Once Ajax and the assassin robots left the chamber, Hammerstein turned to my father said, "Watch on the screen and enjoy the show. Watch as I destroy my creations. I created them. I am their Creator. I am their God. Watch as God destroys his creations."

Hammerstein had a link in the computer chamber to the cameras throughout the facility. He also had a link to the assassin robots. He could see everything in their visual. The feed from the cameras and the robots displayed as a holographic image. It was as if Hammerstein had five huge five-foot-wide color televisions in the chamber.

***

Back outside, Jahvon and I went up to Joshua. We felt nervous. Joshua was about to leave us. We knew that our creator would not let Joshua get to the Washington Monument easily. Jahvon and I feared for his safety. At the same time Joshua knew that Hammerstein would not allow Jahvon, the marines, and me to get to the computer chamber easily. Joshua feared for our safety just as much as we feared for his.

Jahvon said to Joshua, "Run as fast as you can and don't let anything catch you."

Joshua nodded.

Then Jahvon yelled, "Family on three."

Jahvon, Joshua, and I formed a circle, and we each took turns yelling a number. First I yelled, "One," and stuck my hand out in the middle of the circle we made. "Two," Jahvon yelled and stuck his hand out and placed it on top of mine. "Three," Joshua yelled and placed his right hand on top of mine and Jahvon's. Then we all yelled simultaneously, "Family." Then we hugged one another in the circle we made and gave one another light head-butts. That was our way of helping us to get psyched up for what we were about to do: save the world and at the same time face the devil himself, our creator, Nicholas Hammerstein.

***

General Madson yelled, "All right, let's get to it. We got a world to save, people."

President Jamison said, "God speed to all of you. You are all already heroes."

Joshua took a deep breath and, with the pylons in his backpack, took off like a bullet. He was being monitored by the one of the US military drones. He was also given commands in his communication earpiece as to where to run so he would not have a problem finding his way to the Washington Monument.

The SEALs went back to the roof. I was not sure how they were going to get into the facility or where our father was. However, they had the layout of the facility downloaded to them from the command center. This came from Dr. Patel. They were tough warriors in their own right. The ten SEALs quickly scaled the walls and disappeared from view.

Jahvon, the marines, and I stormed into the facility toward the computer chamber. There were marines in front of and behind Jahvon and me. I was the "package," and I had to be protected at all costs. Jahvon was right next to me. We moved as quickly as we could. We did not have Joshua's speed, so it was a challenge for Jahvon and me to keep up with the pace of the marines. We were following the schematics of the facility to where the computer chamber was. We went upstairs and down long corridors. The marines always had their weapons drawn. We traveled up one level and then another until finally we reached the top floor of the facility. The only thing above our location was the roof.

Joshua was running fast. He was not running as fast as he could; he wanted to pace himself. The streets were for the most part blocked off from traffic by the local law enforcement officials. Joshua had close to ten miles to run in now less than twenty-five minutes. Joshua was feeling good. There was nothing to stop him from running to the Washington Monument. Or so he thought.

Joshua got surprised when he heard General Madson yell in a microphone at the command center, "Son, you got company at three o'clock." Joshua heard through his earpiece what the general said but did not know what "at three o'clock" meant. Joshua just assumed it was something behind him. He was right. He looked over his shoulder as he ran and saw two of the Blade of the Shadow killer robots with jetpacks flying toward him about thirty feet in the air. To Joshua they looked like demons from hell, their eyes red, wearing black ninja clothes.

Hammerstein could see what the robots were seeing. He turned to my father, who was also watching the holographic screen, and said, "Your fast son is going to get tired. Meanwhile the Blade of the Shadow will not. They are going to run him down and slaughter him." My father did not make any response. He couldn't. My father still had his mouth gagged with a piece of cloth. Hammerstein did not want a dialogue with my father. He wanted to do all the talking while he kept my father alive. My father's heart sank, seeing those killer robots come after his son. He knew that Hammerstein was correct. Joshua could not run indefinitely without getting tired.

The president and General Madson could see that Joshua was being pursued. The president yelled, "Dammit, can't we get drones to shoot those things down and get them off the kid's back?"

General Madson responded, "No, Mr. President. They are too close to him. If we fire, there is too much risk the boy will be hit as well. He has got to find a way to maneuver away from those things."

The president responded with a frustrated, "Damn."

Joshua was running as fast as he could. Pumping his arms as hard as he could. However, the robots were closing in on him. They stayed on him no matter where he went. Joshua tried running through alleys, underneath buses, through stores, up the walls of buildings. To no avail. All this did was make him more and more tired. Joshua was starting to slow down. He was tiring just as Hammerstein had predicted. Fear in him began to grow as much as fatigue. He knew that it was only a matter of time before the robot monsters caught up to him.

Meanwhile, back inside the facility, Jahvon, the marines, and I made it to the computer chamber.

The corridor leading to the computer room was huge, about thirty feet wide and fifty feet high. At the end of the corridor stood two big double doors. The marine platoon leader let the command center know that we had made it to the computer room. The computer room was very impressive. It was huge. It reminded me of one of those medical classrooms where everything is in circle and the lecturer is in the middle looking up at his students. Except the middle was not at the bottom. Rather the middle was at the top. There were five levels, each about three feet below the next. There were railings on each level. At the top of the level was a control panel where the computer could be operated. I was very impressed with Dr. Patel and sad that Hammerstein had corrupted his work. I ran up the stairs to the fifth level in the chamber and sat in one of the chairs. In the distance at the opposite end of the computer chamber was a door. One of the marines checked it. The door was sealed.

Dr. Patel, who was still patched in to our communications, began to instruct the marines and me how to operate the computer. He told us how to see if its self-destruct had been deactivated.

I told the good doctor that I did not need his instructions. I was able to recognize the technology very easily and knew how to use it. I only needed him to give me the passwords.

After turning on the machine and examining the codes in front of me, I reached an unfortunate conclusion. I told Dr. Patel and all who were within the sound of my voice that indeed the computer's self-destruct mechanism had been not only deactivated but also destroyed. I could tell this by the code readings on the monitor. Dr. Patel was shocked that I, being some twelve-year-old kid, was easily navigating through very sophisticated technology that he had taken a lifetime to master. Now it was confirmed that the only way to activate the self-destruct commands for the satellites was manually.

Everything had to be operated with coding commands. I did need Dr. Patel to give me the five passwords necessary to turn on the manual self-destruct operation of the computer. Dr. Patel gave me the passwords, and I accessed to the self-destruct sequencing. It was amazing. The room filled with numbers from one to nine and zero in yellow holographic forms floating in the air. In front of me appeared very long and very complex math problems. These were problems that were as long as an entire page in an essay. I had to answer each problem in three seconds or less. If I didn't do it, then that problem would disappear and another problem would appear. Only, instead of being closer to completing the self-destruct process, I would be further away. This would cause more time to be lost. Time was not on our side because those satellites were almost fully charged.

I began to answer each question successfully. Dr. Patel, the marines, the president of the United States, and the generals were in awe of how easily I was able to handle these very long and advanced math problems so quickly. It would take the fastest typist at least sixty seconds just to type up these math problems in the most sophisticated computer calculator. Then it would take the best mathematicians in the world about another thirty minutes to figure out the answer. I was doing it all in under three seconds in my head and inputting the answer on a holographic keyboard. The only one present who was not surprised was my brother Jahvon. I felt good about what I was doing, but I knew that I was still going to need that extra fifteen minutes from Joshua. I was praying that he could get the pylons up and running. I could tell the computer was going to throw a lot of questions at me.

The marine commander had posted men at various spots as cover to make sure that none of the Dawn of the Shadow could surprise us from behind. Two men were placed at the head of one of the stairwells that we used in getting to the chamber. Another two were placed at the head of the corridor. Ten took positions in the hallway. The remaining twenty had secured the area outside on the ground. The SEALs left three men atop the facility to keep the roof secure.

Everyone in the computer room was able to see the images of the four satellites. Each satellite had a camera on it to monitor the other satellites. The video feed was sent down to earth to the computer chamber. So I was able to get a live video feed of the satellites in space. The images in the computer room appeared upon the walls of the computer room. Everyone present was in awe of the images.

Then, all of sudden, after I had answered the first couple of questions, we were all horrified to hear gunfire in the distance. Then loud screams by the staircase. Then silence. The screams were the two marines positioned at the staircase leading up to this level. Then we heard more gunfire and screams. It was clear that Dawn of the Shadow was coming. They were coming to stop me from operating the computer. Hammerstein knew that I was the one person who could stop the satellites by activating the self-destruct mechanism.

The marine yelled a command to Jahvon. "Stay with your brother!" Then the marine commander and his troops went to fight whatever evil forces were coming.

Jahvon, breathing heavily from the nervous excitement, turned to me and said, "I got to go help them."

Terrified, I responded, "No, don't leave me alone."

Jahvon yelled back, "Now, look, don't worry. I am going to close that big door and you will be safe in here. Just focus on your math homework."

Jahvon ran out of the computer chamber and, with his superstrength, pulled the three-inch-thick steel doors from left to right. As he was closing the door, with him on the outside, I could see and hear the marines engaged in the battle of their lives. I heard lots of gunfire and the screams of dying marines. I feared for my brother despite his superpowers. Then Jahvon closed the doors with a loud *boom*.

I had to focus on my job. That was solving the math problems. I had to trust and have faith that Jahvon would be able to beat up the bad guys and help the marines.

Outside in the corridor, the marines that were still alive fought a desperate battle against the Blade of the Shadow. The robot monsters fired at the marines, and the marines returned fire. Jahvon jumped over the marines to fight the robots. Bullets harmlessly bounced off him, and he tackled two robots, smashing them into the ground.

Ajax commanded the robots, "Finish the marines first, and then kill the prodigy."

As the command was given, the remaining three robots jumped over Jahvon and ran toward the marines. The bullets of the marines just bounced off the robots. Blades shot from the robots' arms and they cut down each and every marine. One marine took out a flamethrower and blasted one of the robots with flames. All it did was burn away the black ninja-like garment of the robot. The robot assassin then went up to that marine and impaled him on the blade of his arm.

Jahvon was in shock and saddened. The slaughter had happened so quickly, he'd been unable to save any of the marines.

Then Ajax stepped out of the shadows and yelled a command, "Kill the prodigy!"

The three robot assassins surrounded Jahvon. Each fired steel tentacles from its arms. The tentacles seemed alive and wrapped around Jahvon, squeezing him tight. For a moment, Jahvon struggled to even breathe. Then he strained and flexed his muscles as he prepared to break free. The robots then shot currents of powerful electricity through their tentacles into Jahvon. The amount of electricity would easily have killed an ordinary person. But Jahvon was a prodigy. The electric shocks hurt Jahvon. He screamed and dropped to one knee.

In the shadows Ajax was smiling. But Ajax's smile went away as Jahvon slowly stood back up and, resisting the pain of the electric shock, flung his arms open, breaking free of the steel tentacles.

Jahvon then ran to one of the robots and, with a powerful blow from his right hand, punched the head off one of the robots.

Now there were only two of these killer robots left. Another robot's hand turned into a blade and swung down on Jahvon. Jahvon caught the blade and crushed it. Then he grabbed the robot and threw it into the third and final robot with such force that both went flying into the wall and were destroyed.

Jahvon victoriously yelled, "This is *my* house. You hear me, Ajax? You punk. Come out and face me. You evil murdering punk." Jahvon was feeling pumped after destroying the robot assassins. He was ready to give Ajax the beating of his life. At the same time he felt extremely angry and frustrated because, despite all of his powers, he had failed to save the lives of the marines.

Ajax stepped out of the shadows, smiled, and said, "You are indeed powerful, prodigy. It's a shame that you did not work with us at the Dawn of the Shadow. You and your brothers could have killed millions of infidels and joined us in ruling the world. Instead you have failed to meet the purpose for which you were created in the first place. Now you're going to have to die like all the other infidels. Including that fat old man…the owner of the Italian restaurant."

Jahvon gasped and whimpered, "Mr. Ferrante."

Ajax laughed and gleefully said, "Yes, I did not shoot him in the head like the others at the restaurant. I am sure you noticed when you discovered his body that there were no bullet holes. No, no, with him I was slow in killing. I put my hands around his neck and strangled the life out of him." Ajax finished his tale of murder with a dark and an unholy laugh.

189

Jahvon's knuckles cracked as he made a tight fist in anger. He yelled, "Monster!" Jahvon ran toward Ajax, determined to rip him apart for killing a man that he loved as an uncle.

Ajax smiled and stepped back into a shadow.

Then, as Jahvon got closer, a yellowish glow appeared from the shadows in a humanoid form.

Jahvon did not care about the glow. Nothing was going to stop him from smashing Ajax. He got to where Ajax was and threw a punch with his right hand as hard as he could. Only, his mighty blow was stopped in the darkness. Something gripped Jahvon's hand, and he could not pull it free.

How can this be? I have superstrength, Jahvon thought to himself.

Then Ajax stepped out of the shadow with a yellow glowing energy around his body. He was the one holding Jahvon's right fist.

Jahvon was in shock. He wondered how this was possible. *Ajax does not have any superpower,* he thought to himself.

Ajax with a right uppercut punched Jahvon in the body with such power that he flew fifty feet in the air. He crashed into the ceiling and then slammed to the floor of the corridor so that, with one mighty punch, Jahvon suffered three blows.

Dazed and a bit stunned, Jahvon noticed a slight trickle of something coming down from his head. It was something he had never seen before because of his near indestructibility. It was his own blood.

Ajax laughed and said, "What's the matter, prodigy? You never seen your own blood before? No, of course not. How could you? After all you are practically indestructible. Well, all power has its limits. Today I am going to expose yours as I kill you." Then, in his arrogance and belief in his inevitable kill, Ajax offered an explanation as to how he had just battered Jahvon. "You see, this energy glow comes from our technology at the Dawn of the Shadow." He pointed to a small black box on his belt, the size and shape of small cell phone. "We sometimes outsource our technology, like to those stupid terrorists that you defeated at that bank back in New York. The difference here is that I am using the only prototype that allows the energy shield not to be stationary. I am able to cover my whole body with it and move within it. The energy makes me invulnerable to harm and makes me superstrong. In fact, stronger than even you. So fighting me now is going to be just like any twelve-year-old kid going up against a full-grown man. Now, prepare to learn how we beat down infidels in the Dawn of the Shadow."

With his new superstrength—thanks to the energy shield covering his whole body—Ajax leaped thirty feet in the air and flew fifteen feet across the corridor. He came crashing down on Jahvon with such force that he knocked Jahvon through the floor and into the lower levels. About a quarter of the floor came down as well and with it the bodies of the dead marines and the remains of the smashed robot assassins. Ajax landed on top of Jahvon. He grabbed Jahvon by his afro and lifted him up so that Jahvon's feet dangled in the air. Then Ajax with incredible power threw Jahvon through a concrete wall.

Jahvon, despite his near invulnerability, was in a world of hurt. He knew that he could not take this punishment much longer.

Ajax, confident in his certain victory, said, "I could easily smash my way into the computer room and rip the head off that smart brother of yours, but I am having way too much fun with you. Besides, the Creator will take care of your brother and make sure he does not activate the self-destruct mechanism for the satellites."

Jahvon desperately tried to fight Ajax. He charged at him, threw punches at Ajax. Ajax easily blocked them like a grown man would block the blows of a child.

Then Ajax smashed Jahvon in his face, knocking him again into a wall and busted Jahvon's nose. Another blow gave Jahvon a black eye.

Ajax was indeed having fun. He liked to take his time with a kill. As he pummeled Jahvon, Ajax bragged about his career as a killer. About how he had killed and tortured men, women, and children in service to the Dawn of the Shadow. He talked about how he had brutalized our father over twelve years ago and how much he had enjoyed it.

Jahvon fell into despair as his body was battered and bloodied by this hardcore career killer.

On one of the screens in the communication room, my father and Hammerstein could see Ajax punishing Jahvon. My father's heart sank, seeing another son's life potentially coming to an end. Hammerstein enjoyed the new entertainment that Ajax was providing him.

In the computer room, I was unaware of what was transpiring. I had noticed only that, after hearing loud noises and screams, the noise had stopped. Little did I know that Jahvon was engaged in mortal combat with Ajax.

Over and over again I answered each and every math question that was thrown at me. As I answered each question, my confidence grew. I knew in my heart that I could do this. I also knew that I was going to need as much time as possible. I said a silent prayer to myself that Joshua would be able to get me that extra fifteen minutes.

Then out of nowhere I heard the voice of Hammerstein, my creator. There was a speaker in the computer room somewhere on the ceiling. Hammerstein and my father were watching me on one of the large holographic screens in the communication room. Just as they watched Ajax pummeling Jahvon. Just as they watched

Joshua hotly pursued by two of Blade of the Shadow robots.

Hammerstein now attacked something that I desperately needed to activate the self-destruct mechanism: my confidence.

Over the speaker, Hammerstein said, "Tell me, prodigy, how does it feel to be a loser? You are a loser. Just like your father. He never amounted to anything. And you, despite your intellect, will never amount to anything. You're just a failed experiment. You are not even human. You are a *freak*. I enjoyed killing your father's SEAL team twelve years ago. I enjoyed torturing him back them. I am enjoying torturing him now. You and your daddy are nothing to me. You don't have what it takes to destroy the satellites. Why? Because you are a loser like your pathetic daddy. You were created to dominate the world, but instead you and your father were in hiding for the past twelve years like scared rats."

Hammerstein went on and on with his taunts. His goal was to break my concentration and attack my confidence. It was working. His taunts about my dad and me were getting to me. I was losing my confidence. My concentration failed. This manifested in me getting questions wrong that I should have answered correctly. Soon, I was getting them all wrong.

Yes, I was brilliant with superintelligence, but I was still a kid. And any kid needs confidence to do a task no matter how talented he is.

My confidence grew weaker and weaker. I got more and more questions wrong. And as I got more questions wrong, my confidence weakened even more. It was a vicious psychological cycle, my failure feeding upon itself, and I was mentally and emotionally trapped by it.

It was exactly what that evil mastermind had intended.

Dr. Patel, the president, and the national security team felt a sense of despair. They were monitoring my progress and could see that I had gone from answering all the questions correctly to now answering all the questions incorrectly. They did not understand why. They of course could not hear what Hammerstein was doing. They could only read what the computer was doing remotely from Dr. Patel's monitoring technology.

Back outside, Joshua was running for his life from the two killer robots. Though he was getting closer to the Washington Monument, he was slowing down considerably. Thanks to the raw speed of their jetpacks, the robots now had the advantage. Joshua felt his only hope was to do more maneuvers. He ran into and through stores, hotels, and homes—anywhere he might lose the assassin robots. Nothing was working. Joshua's breathing grew heavier and heavier. He felt like his heart was going to pump out of his chest. Finally, he had no choice. He ran into an underground parking lot. The robots pursued him. They landed on the ground, and their mechanical hands retracted and folded into their forearms. Then out of their forearms came minibarrels. Anyone looking at this would find it obvious that some type of firearm was going to be discharged from those barrels. The robots began shooting minirockets out of their forearms. Joshua tried to hide between and under cars. However, the explosions of the cars chased him out of hiding. There was an incredible amount of destruction in the parking lot. The robots were trying to use their firepower to guide Joshua into the open so they could finish him. He scrambled to get behind any cover he could find. Fortunately, this was a huge parking lot. It had a lot of cars. Flames engulfed the parking lot, and the assassin robots blocked the exit. They also made sure to destroy the entrance to the staircase so Joshua could not escape. There were no openings. The only way for Joshua to leave was the way he came in. However, that was being blocked by the Blade of the Shadow.

Joshua was able to get behind a row of twenty cars, breathing extremely heavily. An endless amount of sweat ran from his body. He felt weak because he was starving. Most of all he was scared to death of being blown to bits by the robots.

The assassin robots knew exactly where he was—behind a blue van, the last vehicle in the row. The robots decided to blast and destroy each vehicle so Joshua could not use them as cover. They knew in their inhuman minds that Joshua would emerge eventually, and then they would finish him.

Joshua was in the corner, cowering in fear, so exhausted that he gasped for each breath. He just could not run anymore. In despair, he believed it was only a matter of time before he would die. He felt shame for failing to do his part in fighting the Dawn of the Shadow; he had failed to get the pylons to the proper location.

Chapter 15

Our Greatest Hero

Back in the communications center, Hammerstein was enjoying the show. Not only could he see Ajax pummeling Jahvon and me getting the math problems all wrong, now he was watching what seemed to be the inevitable death of Joshua. Hammerstein was able to get a visual of what was going on in the parking lot.

Tears fell from my father's eyes as he watched in silence what was happening to us, his sons, whom he loved dearly.

Hammerstein was not done. He wanted to make sure that there was no chance of me completing the necessary math problems to activate the self-destruct for the satellites. He set up a highly sophisticated camera facing my father. Then he took a small vial of green liquid from his pouch and drew his twelve-inch dagger, the same dagger that he had used to impale and kill many of my father's friends. He poured the green liquid on the blade. Then he turned to my father, still chained to the wall and gagged, badly beaten and bloody.

"As you can see from the holographic screens, Jordan, your sons have been defeated. Ajax is beating one to death. The Blade of the Shadow are about to blow another to hell. As for the smart one, well, he may not die right now, but his confidence is destroyed. That smart one is the only one I feared. What I am about to do is make sure that there is no chance of his confidence ever coming back to complete the task of destroying those satellites. I am going to kill you, Jordan. And I am going to record it and send it to him so he can see." Hammerstein spoke in a tone of mock sadness. "Seeing his daddy stabbed with a poisoned blade...well, that will be *so* traumatic for the little fellow. He'll never be able to concentrate after seeing his daddy dealt a death blow. You see this green solution, Jordan? It comes from a very poisonous snake in the Amazon. It will kill you for sure and there is no cure. The good news is it won't be swift. I made some modifications to the poison because I don't want you dying quick. I want your heart filled with sadness before it stops beating. It will take a little bit of time before you die. This way you will be able to enjoy the show of the satellites coming down upon the earth, killing millions. But not before seeing two of your sons die and the third fail to save the world."

Hammerstein went up to my father with the blade in his hand and the minicamera rolling. He grabbed my father by the throat and triumphantly said, "You took my prodigies away from me twelve years ago. Now I am taking you away from them. I told you twelve years ago, Jordan, that I would find you and make you pay. I told you I was going to kill you. Well, this is me keeping my promise to you."

My father and Hammerstein looked at each other, and their eyes locked. Both feeling hatred toward the other, just as they had when they did battle twelve years ago. Only this time Hammerstein had the advantage. My father knew there was nothing he could do to stop his enemy from plunging that blade into him.

However, as he looked into my father's eyes, Hammerstein knew he was looking into the eyes of an enemy who was not afraid of death. An enemy whose spirit Hammerstein had never broken, despite breaking his body. Hammerstein finally took the dagger filled with the poison and plunged it into my father. My father let out a muffled scream. As Hammerstein had promised, the blow was not immediately fatal. He had driven the blade in just deep enough for the poison to begin making its way into the bloodstream. Almost immediately my father felt its effect.

Hammerstein laughed victoriously. Today he would both change the world and kill his enemy.

Hammerstein's celebration was violently interrupted by an explosion from the ceiling. His men and Hammerstein started shooting upward, engaged suddenly in a fierce gunfight.

It was the Navy SEALs. They had found the location of the communications chamber. The soldiers of the Dawn of the Shadow were excellent marksmen. But they were no match for the marksmanship of the Navy SEALs. One by one the soldiers of the Dawn of the Shadow fell, killed by the Navy SEALs.

Hammerstein seized the camera he had used to record my father's murder. Then, with incredible athletic speed for a man in his sixties and firing his handgun at the SEALs, he fought his way through an opening in the back of the communications chamber.

The SEALs killed the last of Hammerstein's men and jumped down to pursue him.

However, Hammerstein closed the sliding door behind him and managed to lock it. The Navy SEALs were not able to pursue him.

Hammerstein yelled through the door at my father, "Good-bye, Jordan. Enjoy your last few hours on earth. Don't worry, your children will be joining you soon."

The Navy SEALs and my father heard Hammerstein's loud laughter fade as he fled.

The SEALs cleared and secured the room. They shot the chains holding my father. My father, in his damaged and poisoned body, fell helplessly into the arms of two of the Navy SEALs. They gently lowered him to the ground. The SEALs knew that my father was not just some hostage they were here to rescue. He was one of their own. He was himself a SEAL. That in itself created a bond between him and this Seal team.

They laid him on the ground to try to stop the bleeding from the stab wound.

"Hang on, soldier," the SEAL commander said. "You are going to be just fine. We are going to get you out."

Lying in pain on the ground, knowing he was going to die, my father reached up and grabbed the shoulder of the SEAL commander. He looked at the holographic screens showing my brothers and me and said, "Did you establish communication with my sons?"

"Yes, soldier. We did," the SEAL commander said. "Each one has an earpiece that I secured myself. Those are some incredible kids you have there. Now we've got to get you out of here. Those are our orders. And we made a promise to your boys that we're going to keep."

My father smiled through battered lips and said, "You need to delay that promise and that order. There's something I need you to do or millions are going to die." He then whispered a request to the SEAL.

Meanwhile another SEAL used his communication device to call central command to report to the generals and the president: "We secured the room, and we have the father in custody. Hammerstein has escaped, and we are not able to pursue. Over."

General Madson responded: "Are you able to secure the machine controlling the satellites?"

"The controls seem locked, sir. Sending a visual now."

The SEAL used a small video camera to provide a live feed to the central command. This was then sent to Dr. Patel, who would be able to determine what was going on. There was a hope that, since the SEALs had managed to take over the communications room, perhaps they could find a way to control or stop the satellites with Dr. Patel's guidance.

Dr. Patel looked at that monitors on the communications panel and instructed the SEALs as to what to do.

After two intense minutes, it grew clear to Dr. Patel that their efforts would not work. He shared his grim understanding of the situation: "Mr. President, it appears that the controls are locked. Meaning we cannot override any of the satellites. The news gets much worse I am afraid." Dr. Patel took a very deep breath and then spoke with his heart in his throat. "Based on my readings of the satellites, and in looking at the commands on the control panel monitors, the satellites will destroy Washington. And they have been programmed to target and cause the same destruction in all fifty states. Hammerstein does not need to manually control the satellites. He managed to program the commands of destruction within them. One by one, each and every state in the union will burn over the next twenty-four hours. Close to 300 million people will die. It appears that monster Hammerstein thought of every contingency."

"Dear God," replied the president. His were the only words at that moment. Everyone else was in too much shock to speak.

Dr. Patel said, "Our only hope is if those 'kids' are successful in carrying out our original plan."

Everyone within the sound of Dr. Patel's voice felt a severe sense of dread. Far worse than they had felt before. I was no longer answering the math questions. My confidence had been too damaged by the words of Hammerstein. Jahvon was being thrown around like a rag doll by Ajax. And Joshua was about to be killed by the killer robots in an underground parking lot. Our failures were on display on the holographic screens in the communication chamber. The "original plan" was not working.

All hope seemed lost. Millions of innocents were about to die. Evil was on the verge of absolute victory. Only twenty minutes remained before the satellites unleashed their powerful fury upon the earth, starting with Washington. Panic was in the streets. Fear spread across the country and around the world. The president and his national security team had no answers. Somewhere the evil High Masters of the Dawn of the Shadow were watching and laughing. Their dark dream was about to become a reality.

When it seemed as if the world as we knew it was about to end and evil would reign, a miracle happened. No, not a miracle, rather, a hero happened. A hero at that moment rose up with the help of two Navy SEALs under each of his arms. Battered, bloodied, dying, but *determined*. It was that same hero who rescued my brothers and me from the hands of evil over twelve years ago. It was the same hero who kept my brothers and me safe. The same hero who fought for us. The same hero who fed us. The same hero who kept us clean. The same hero who gave us shelter. The same hero who taught us about life and about ourselves. The same hero who taught us right from wrong. The same hero who laughed with us. The same hero who put a smile on our faces when we would cry. The same hero who was patient with us even when we frustrated him. This was the very same hero who, even in his weakened condition, was now the one who rose up to save us. Not with superstrength. Not with superspeed. Not with superintelligence. No, on this day he saved me, my brothers, and millions of other lives with the power and inspiration of his love. This hero was the greatest hero my brothers and I had ever known. This was the greatest hero we would ever know. This hero was our father, *our greatest hero*.

The president and national security team watched the SEALs lifting my father up to standing position. Then one of the SEALs pressed some buttons on a portable communication device, the same device that allowed the SEALs to communicate with my brothers and me.

My brothers and I heard a *ping* sound in our earpieces.

General Madson asked the SEALs, "What is going on?"

The SEAL commander smiled and said, "It's simple, sir. We are just letting a father talk to his kids." The SEAL commander raised a small microphone to my father's mouth as he was being held up by the two SEALs. "You're up, soldier."

Then my father looked up at each of us and saw the troubles that we were having. He saw Jahvon battered and bloodied, crawling on the ground, while in the distance a smiling Ajax walked toward him. He saw Joshua still gasping for breath while two of the Blade of the Shadow were shooting and blowing up vehicles one by one to get to him. He saw me with my face in my hands, frustrated at not being able to answer any more questions because all the confidence had been taken out of me. It was clear that Hammerstein did know exactly how to beat his creations. However, these prodigies were not just the creation of a madman. They were *my father's children*. His sons. And although Hammerstein knew how to take his creations down, my father knew how to lift his sons up.

Daddy took a deep breath and spoke words in the microphone that everyone within the sound of his voice would remember for the rest of their lives. "Boys...boys. Jason...Jahvon...Joshua. It's me. It's Daddy."

My brothers and I were startled to all of sudden hear our father's voice through our earpieces. Just the sound of his voice helped us feel better.

We each said, "Daddy? Daddy!" Not knowing he had been poisoned, we each felt some comfort that the SEALs had kept their word and rescued our father from Hammerstein.

Daddy continued, "Boys, listen. I don't have a lot of time to talk. Just listen." He looked up at each of us on the holographic screens. "I...know you are scared. I know you're hurt. That's OK, that's OK. That's what happens in life; sometimes it makes you scared and it hurts you. The challenges of life can even take away your confidence. You have to overcome that. You have to. It's not your powers that make you heroes. It's your willingness to help others and do the right thing even when things are the most difficult in your lives. Even when you are scared and hurt and your confidence is shaken.

"Hammerstein was right. Yes, you are indeed prodigies. But you are prodigies of good. Prodigies of making the world a better place. Prodigies of standing up for what is right. You are my prodigies, mine. And I believe in you. But...you...you...have to also believe in yourselves. Remember, remember the lessons that I taught each of you individually. Use those lessons now...and I guarantee you...will...win. Now get up. Don't give up. Believe in yourselves. Fight for what's right." My father paused for a brief moment then his voice filled with even more emotion than before. "Most of all, my beautiful, wonderful sons, Joshua, Jason, and Jahvon, always remember that when you fight, I fight with you. And never, ever, ever forget that I love you...with all of my heart, now and forever." He yelled into the microphone, "*Now...go...beat...these...bad guys...up!*"

My brothers and I said from our respective locations, "Love you too, Daddy."

My father, emotionally and physically exhausted, collapsed upon the conclusion of his speech. The SEALs gently lowered him to the floor as they called a military helicopter to their location for an evacuation. The fifth satellite was no longer a threat since they had taken over the communications chamber.

Chapter 16

Victory

Words cannot adequately describe the effect that our father's words had on Jahvon, Joshua, and me. Hearing his words was like electricity going through our bodies. It was an electricity of inspiration. The exact kind of inspiration that we each needed at the exact moment that we needed it. Each of us clenched our fists. We were all still scared. But thanks to our father's words, we each knew we were going to find a way to overcome our individual challenges. We each felt the same obligation. That was to not let our father down.

We each did as our father had instructed us to do. Simultaneously, we each remembered his lessons and his love for us.

Joshua was still breathing heavy. His heart was pumping so fast and hard that it felt like it would come out of his chest. The sounds of exploding vehicles grew closer and closer as the assassin robots wielded their firepower. Joshua closed his eyes. He did as my father instructed. He remembered Daddy's lessons for him specifically. Joshua remembered the time we were in the Pocono Mountains. He remembered the lesson that Daddy taught about the martial arts. He remembered how this lesson helped him with his running. Daddy had told him that the most important part of martial arts is the breathing. You must be able to master your breathing. By mastering your breathing, you can control your energy. By controlling your energy, you can control your body, even slow down your heartbeat. And by slowing your heartbeat, you can get your second wind. Joshua closed his eyes. He blocked out the noise of the explosions that were getting closer and closer to him. He then stood up, still behind the van. He took a deep breath. As he inhaled, he kept his hands by his side and then raised his hands up toward his armpits, with palms facing up. As he raised his hands, he inhaled. Then when he could lift his hands no higher, he turned his palms downward and slowly exhaled. Just as Daddy taught him. He repeated this process four more times. Joshua's heartbeat was starting to slow. He was doing something that he could not do moments before. He was getting control of his breathing. Then, when he had gained further control of his breathing, he did a karate kata called *Sanchin kata*. This kata entailed a lot of deep breathing. This allowed him to have even more control of his breathing, until finally he got his second wind. Now he was prepared to start running again.

Just before our father's speech, Jahvon had just been thrown forty feet into a wall by Ajax. Jahvon laying on the ground, hurt remembered Daddy's lesson to him. The lesson that Daddy had given him the day they were collecting wood.

On that day Daddy had asked him what he would do if he faced and enemy who was stronger than he was. What he would do if he encountered an enemy who laughed at his superstrength? On that day Jahvon had no answers. My father told him that Jahvon was not some dumb brute. My father told him that he was smart. Real smart. Then my father told him that his greatest weapon was not his superstrength; his greatest weapon was his *mind*. He told him that when you face a powerful enemy, just like in life, you must use your *head*.

I was still in the computer chamber. I remembered the lesson that Daddy had given me. I remembered the day I told him how I was jealous of my brothers. How I wished I had superspeed or superstrength. I remembered him telling me how I was a master of mathematics. How there was nothing in the world that I couldn't do. I remembered him telling me how he believed in me, but that I must also believe in myself. I remembered him saying I was wrong to be jealous of my brothers. That they instead should be jealous of me. With these memories of the lessons from my father, I was able to regain the confidence that Hammerstein's stinging words had taken from me. I once again began to answer the math questions that the computer was generating. Again, as I answered each question correctly, my confidence grew stronger and stronger.

Back in the underground parking lot, Joshua stepped out from where he had hidden behind the van. He looked at the robot assassins and said, "OK, bad guys, let's play tag."

The robot assassins opened fire on him.

Joshua ran in a defensive pattern around the robots' location in the parking lot. The bullets and rockets fired at him missed. The sounds of gunfire ricocheting echoed behind him as well as the sounds of exploding rockets. Then Joshua quickly ran past the robots toward the exit. The robots again gave pursuit. Once Joshua had drawn the robots out of the parking facility, they became visible to the military. But the military concluded that they could not fire upon the robots because they were too close to Joshua. All they could do was follow in the air with two military helicopters. Joshua spotted the helicopters and, as he ran, figured that they could not fire upon the robots because they were flying too close to him. The robots were flying low and fast, only about ten feet behind Joshua and closing in. Joshua tried to lose them like he did before. But the robots stayed with him. As they flew, their hands retracted into their forearms. In their place, out popped twenty-four-inch blades. They were not going to try to shoot Joshua while they were in pursuit. They intended to cut him down.

Joshua knew that he could not get to the Washington Monument before they cut him into pieces. He was once again starting to get tired. His second wind was coming to an end. He could feel it in his lungs. Then Joshua decided to do something unexpected. He slowed down to let the robots get extremely close to him. Once they were within three feet, he made a sudden stop. When he did, one of the robots swung its blade at Joshua's neck. Joshua made sure to duck. The robots could not stop their forward momentum as quickly as he could. They flew over and past Joshua, trying to chop his head off. Then Joshua spun and ran back in the direction he'd come from. President Jamison, General Madson, the national security team, and the other military persons were all surprised by what they saw.

The president yelled, "Dammit, he is running in the wrong direction."

Then General Madson said, "Look, sir, the boy is yelling something."

The general then had a report from one of the Black Hawk helicopters that was now in front of Joshua.

Joshua slowed down and yelled to the military, "Shoot at me! Shoot at me!" The snipers in the choppers who had Joshua in their scopes could not hear what he said, but they were able to read his lips, and they recognized the sign of a gun he made with his hand and pointed at himself.

With hesitation, one of the military personnel reported to General Madson what he believed Joshua was saying.

The president asked the question that everyone was thinking at that moment: "Why in the hell would this kid want us to shoot him?"

Then General Madson looked at how close the robots were to him on the screen. The snipers and the Black Hawk helicopters were in front of Joshua at a distance of about three hundred feet. And that distance was decreasing. Then it became clear to the general what Joshua wanted to do.

To everyone's surprise, General Madson gave an order to the military units manning the Black Hawk helicopters. "Target that boy and fire your weapons now with everything you got."

The president said, "General, what the hell are you doing? That kid is the only one who can get the pylons to the Washington Monument. Why in the hell are you trying to kill him?"

The general nervously said, "I am not, sir. I am trying to help him."

The military helicopters targeted Joshua with their weapons. Red dots appeared on Joshua's head and torso as he ran. The robots were closing in on him. They were now only about five feet away. Joshua knew the helicopters were about to fire upon him. He remembered the lesson that Daddy gave him about dodging bullets. He had told him that he had the ability to slow down the world around him. One of the robots was now right behind him. Close enough to chop Joshua's head off. The robot assassin raised its arms in anticipation of delivering the killing blow to Joshua. Then the military helicopters fired. Hundreds of rounds of bullets flew through the air. Joshua sidestepped, ducked, and dodged each and every bullet that came near him. Fortunately, the robots could not dodge as effectively. The robots were blasted by hundreds of bullets each. The rounds coming from the military were stronger than the ones that had come from the marines earlier. In addition, there were far more rounds being fired from the machinery from the helicopters. The bodies of the robots literally exploded in the air.

Once it was clear that the robots were destroyed, the general yelled, "Cease fire."

The military units complied with the command.

The president of the United States said to General Madson, "How did you know the kid would do that?"

The general said, "I didn't. I just had faith."

Joshua was now free of being pursued. Joshua then did a very short kata that took about ten seconds, took some deep breaths, and ran back toward the Washington Monument. Only five minutes were left before the satellites exploded down upon the earth. Joshua had five miles to go to get to the Washington Monument. He ran as hard as he could. He remembered Daddy's words as he ran: "Running is more than just a talent. There is also technique to it. Control your breathing and pump your arms. The harder you pump your arms, the faster you will go." Joshua ran and ran and ran. The national security team, watching him from a drone satellite, marveled at his speed.

The president yelled at the screen, "Go, go, go, go!"

General Madson himself yelled, "C'mon, c'mon!"

These men, who before today had never seen or were even aware of Joshua, found themselves now rooting for him. Joshua was mindful as he ran that millions were about to die. Once again his heart pumped faster in his chest because of the amount he was pushing his body. Despite this, he was determined not to stop, even if it killed him. He closed the distance from five miles away to four. Then from three miles to two. Now he only had a mile to go, and less than ninety seconds to get there.

He saw the blue flare in the distance and the marines who were waiting for him. They would operate the pylons he was carrying. Sweat poured down his face. His pants were ripped to shreds from the running. The soles of his sneakers were almost worn through. But Joshua did not stop. He kept going until finally he ran into the arms of two marines. They gently lowered him to ground and took the pylons from his backpack. They placed the pylons on the ground and pressed the blue buttons. Out of the pylons came a colorful blue energy that shot up into the sky. The blue energy climbed thirty thousand feet into the air then spread outward, widening into a dome that was miles wide.

It was just in time. The four primary satellites erupted down upon the earth. It seemed as if the sun itself was exploding. The amount of raw power that the sattelites unleashed was truly spectacular. What was even more incredible was that the blue energy acted as a shield against such power. Seeing the satellite blast upon the shield was just as awesome and terrible to watch.

Dr. Patel yelled, "Thank God, the shield is holding. It's holding."

General Madson said, "That kid just got millions of people fifteen more minutes of life. Now it's up to his brother to finish the math problems to activate the self-destruct on the satellites."

The marines with Joshua gave him an oxygen mask to help him recover because they could see that he was desperate for each breath. As Joshua inhaled, he thought to himself that he had to get back to the facility to help Jahvon and me. But first he needed a few minutes to breathe deeply the oxygen and restore himself.

It was indeed a victory for Joshua. He had done his job and got the pylons where they needed to go. He had saved, at least temporarily, the lives of millions of people who would have been incinerated. Now it was up to me to get the self-destruct mechanism activated. As I was in the chamber, I could see on one of the monitors that the satellites had erupted upon the earth. I also saw a timer of fifteen minutes come up on the monitor. When I spotted the countdown, I felt really good. I felt good because I knew Joshua had delivered the pylons to where they needed to go. I also knew that, based on the momentum I had answering the math problems, the extra fifteen minutes were all I would need to activate the self-destruct for each of the four satellites. *We're doing it. We're saving the day,* I thought. I had a huge smile on my face and extreme confidence in myself. My brothers and I were going to be heroes. Little did I know that at that moment our creator, Hammerstein, was not finished carrying out his evil plans.

***

At the same time that Joshua was doing his running, back at the facility, Jahvon was still dealing with the problem of Ajax trying to kill him. Jahvon had turned around, still on the ground, and faced Ajax. Ajax slowly marched toward him, smiling, laughing at what he thought was an inevitable kill. Jahvon looked closely at Ajax, who was about thirty feet away. He looked at the glowing energy covering Ajax's body. He remembered Ajax's words about how this weapon that he was using against Jahvon was a prototype. Based on the technology that the Dawn of the Shadow outsourced to terrorists like the ones that Jahvon faced at the bank. Jahvon also remembered how that technology was defeated at the bank. *Shown to him by me,* Jahvon thought. The only difference between the technology that created the field surrounding the bomb that the terrorists had in the bank and the technology that Ajax now wielded was the fact that in Ajax's case the energy field surrounded his body, allowing him to move and fight within it's shield. But that was it. And if that was the only difference, Jahvon thought, then he could destroy this energy field—just as he had seen me destroy the energy field in the bank.

Armed with these thoughts in his mind, Jahvon leaped over Ajax with his powerful legs and landed behind him.

Ajax, frustrated, yelled, "Stand and fight, coward."

Jahvon then ran to the dead body of one of the marines killed earlier by the Blade of the Shadow, the one with the flamethrower.

Ajax ran at Jahvon as quickly as he could, with hatred in his eyes.

Jahvon got to one knee to remove the flamethrower's handle from the grip of the deceased marine. Then Jahvon pointed the flamethrower at Ajax and pulled the flamethrower's trigger. With a loud *phoosh*, a ball of fire erupted from the flamethrower, engulfing Ajax.

Ajax paused for a momment as the flames engulfed him. He was slightly surprised, but in his mind, this was a harmless attack. He laughed and said, "Fool, this shield protects me from all harm. Did you really think it would stop me from killing you?" He continued to come toward Jahvon, unharmed by the flames.

Jahvon did not expect the flames to harm Ajax. However, he was looking for another reaction to the flames, one that would indicate the strategy was working. Then it happened. Just as it did at the bank when flames hit the glowing energy that had protecting the bomb. The flames caused the glow around Ajax to turn red. Now Jahvon knew that his strategy was working. Again he ran away from Ajax.

Again Ajax yelled, "Coward!"

Jahvon spotted a fire hose on the wall. With his superstrength, he smashed the glass and pulled the fire hose out. Ajax again was racing toward him. Jahvon feared that he was running out of time. He could not avoid Ajax forever. His plan had better work, or eventually Ajax would catch him and pummel him to death.

Jahvon turned the water on and walked about twenty feet to fully stretch out the hose. Normally such a hose required the strength of three or four strong men to hold it. But for Jahvon it was no problem.

Ajax ran headlong into the powerful blast of water coming out of the hose. He was not at all bothered thanks to the strength that the energy field gave him. The blast would have knocked over a normal man. For Ajax, it was amusing. He marched his way through the gushing water and knocked Jahvon to the ground with a powerful backhand swing of his right arm.

Jahvon cried out from the blow and looked up from the ground at Ajax standing over him. His plan had worked. The shield around Ajax had changed color, from glowing yellow to glowing red and now to glowing blue.

Ajax, who was not at all concerned with the color of the energy shield, stood triumphantly over Jahvon and said, "Now I am going to smash you even worse than I did your stupid daddy twelve years ago. And I am going to kill you worse than I did that fat Italian." He lifted his right fist in the air. Then, with all his might, he threw that fist down upon the head of Jahvon.

Bam! was the loud sound from the blow. However, it was not what Ajax had expected; the blow had not struck Jahvon's head. Instead, with his left hand Jahvon had caught the powerful blow in midair.

With surprise, Ajax discovered that he could not pull his hand back from Jahvon's grip. He tried, but despite his strength and the strength that the technology had given him, he could not do it.

Now Jahvon had placed Ajax in the same position that Ajax had put him in when their fight first began. Jahvon rose to his feet, still holding Ajax's right fist. The tide of the battle had turned, and both combatants knew it.

Ajax, astonished by what was happening, said, "How is this possible?"

Jahvon replied, "It's simple. You didn't read the instruction manual."

Then Jahvon clenched his hand around Ajax's, and the now-blue energy field began to crack. Ajax gasped.

Jahvon said, "Now you are going to learn how we beat down bad guys in Brooklyn." With his right hand, Jahvon threw a powerful straight punch into Ajax's stomach.

With a loud *boom*, Ajax flew twenty feet backward into a wall. The blow put another crack in his energy shield. But while the shield was now split in two places, Ajax was still unharmed and strong. He believed he still had enough superstrength, thanks to the energy field, to defeat this little infidel in combat. Ajax would soon discover just how wrong he was.

Jahvon charged Ajax, Ajax charged Jahvon, and the two combatants collided with a *whoom*, as if two trains had smashed into each other. Unfortunately for Ajax, his was the inferior train. Jahvon knocked him backward, causing more cracks in the energy shield. It was clear that field was not as strong as it was before. It was also clear that it could not take much more punishment from Jahvon's power.

Jahvon intended to take full advantage of that. He grabbed Ajax by the left ankle, swung him over his head, and slammed him onto the ground. He did it again and again: *Bam! Bam! Bam!* With each impact, more and more cracks spread through Ajax's shield, until it looked like a big jigsaw puzzle.

Jahvon then put Ajax into a headlock with his left hand. Ajax was not strong enough to get Jahvon off him. With his right hand, Jahvon punched Ajax over and over again in the head. *Bam, bam! Bap, bap! Boom, boom!* More and more cracks appeared in the shield. Jahvon then let Ajax out of the headlock. He wanted to look his enemy in the face because he truly believed the end for Ajax was near. Jahvon held Ajax by the shoulder and said, "This is for hurting my daddy!" He threw a punch with his right hand at Ajax's face. *Boom!* "This is for threatening the lives of millions!" Another right-hand punch struck Ajax's face. *Boom!*

By now, the shield looked ready to disintegrate. But not before Jahvon got off one more punch.

"And this, you monster, is for Mr. Ferrante!" With all his might, Jahvon threw a right uppercut into Ajax's stomach. *Bam!* The sound echoed throughout the facility, and the blow was so powerful it sent Ajax flying forty feet to the ceiling.

Upon impact with the ceiling, the energy shield finally gave. It shattered into a dozen little glowing pieces and evaporated into the air.

Now, without the protection of the shield, Ajax fell forty feet to the ground. The impact fractured his left arm and right leg. Ajax also broke a few ribs in the fall.

Jahvon had done it. He defeated a hardcore killer. Most importantly, he'd done it with his intellect, just as Daddy had taught him. Now it was Jahvon standing triumphantly over Ajax. Now it was Ajax who was battered and bloodied in defeat. Jahvon grabbed him by the throat and lifted Ajax up to eye level. Without the energy shield, Ajax had no chance against Jahvon's superstrength. The fact that Ajax was hurt only made it worse for him. The once-mighty Ajax was helpless.

Jahvon squeezed his neck. "So tell me, bad guy, how does it feel to die by being strangled? The same way you killed Mr. Ferrante."

Ajax said nothing. He felt the powerful grip of Jahvon slowly crushing his neck. Ajax's life was about to end.

Then, as he saw Ajax's eyes roll back in his head, Jahvon let him go.

Ajax fell to the ground, coughing for breath, his throat too compressed to breathe.

Ajax laughed through his bloody lips and tauntingly said to Jahvon, "What's the matter, boy? You were created to kill. You don't have the guts to do it? You really are a failed freak of nature."

In anger Jahvon then grabbed Ajax by the neck again, only this time with just enough pressure to hold him securely without the risk of strangling him. "I am not a killer. That's not the path that my daddy taught me. I don't need to kill you. Beating you up is good enough for me. And I am proud of that."

Ajax again laughed. Then he said, "You may have defeated me, but your brother still has not activated the self-destruct mechanism on the satellites. Nothing is going to stop the satellites from coming down to earth and killing millions. How long do you think the pylons, if activated, are going to hold? Fifteen minutes at most. Face it, boy. You may have defeated me, but the Dawn of the Shadow has still won."

Even in defeat, Ajax's words gave Jahvon a chill down his spine.

He had achieved a great victory, but the lives of millions were still at risk.

C'mon, Jason, he thought, with Ajax's neck still in his grip, *please do your math homework.*

Chapter 17

Final Battle

Since Hammerstein was no longer in control of the communications chamber, thanks to the Navy SEALs, he no longer had control over the fifth satellite. Therefore, the fifth satellite was no longer an immediate threat to any aircraft that came close to the facility. However, the US military could not destroy the facility because that would not have stopped the four prime satellites from blasting the earth. Only I could stop them, by activating the self-destruct mechanism from the main computer chamber.

The good news was that now rescue helicopters could evacuate the SEALs and my father. They arrived after my father's speech. The military helicopters shot rockets to the roof of the facility and created a ten-foot-wide hole. The SEALs then made sure my dad had stopped bleeding and readied him for an airlift evacuation. The helicopter lowered a stretcher. After my dad was placed in the stretcher he was lifted gently up to the chopper. The other SEALs then followed. Two of the SEALs remained to evacuate Jahvon and me, if necessary.

While Jahvon was battling Ajax, and the military was getting our father out, I was busy answering all the complex math problems. Even though Jahvon was worried about my progress, I felt good about what I was doing. With the extra fifteen minutes, I knew that there was nothing to stop me from doing my part in saving the lives of millions of people and stopping our creator.

What I did not know at the time was that Hammerstein was not done trying to stop me. When Hammerstein had escaped the SEALs, he made his way through a passage toward the computer room where I was. The computer room and the two big double doors had been sealed. However, a smaller door also led to the computer room. The passageway that Hammerstein was taking led to that door. Hammerstein knew I was in the computer room alone, and he intended to cut my throat from ear to ear. Fortunately, that door was also closed and locked. Hammerstein tried to kick the door open. He tried shooting the lock. Luckily, for me, the door held. I heard the kicking and the gunfire from the door. I did not know who it was initially. Finally, Hammerstein revealed that it was he behind the door. He began to taunt me again. He called me a failure and a loser. I kept thinking of the speech that my father had given a few minutes earlier. I was still riding that positive adrenaline rush of inspiration. But Hammerstein was not about to give up.

Hammerstein had a handheld device where he could upload information to the main computer at the facility. He did not have the technology to stop me, but he did have the ability to send me communications, including video communications.

He said from behind the door, "You are going to fail, boy. You are not going to stop the satellites from erupting."

I responded, "Oh, yes I am. In fact, I am almost done, you monster."

Time was running out. I had about five more minutes left before the energy from the satellites blasted through energy field created by the pylons.

Then the madman took the device that was connected to the camera that he'd used to video himself stabbing my father. He then attached that device to another handheld device.

Then the madman said to me, "Poison from a death adder snake."

I paused for a split second and wondered why he would say that. What did poison from a death adder snake, which I was familiar with, have to do with what was going on now?

Then Hammerstein pressed a white button on the handheld device that he'd attached from the camera.

My dad appeared on one of the screens in the chamber. I saw him chained and battered. This caused me to stop answering the math questions. The president, the president's staff, the generals, and Dr. Patel could see on their equipment that I had stopped answering questions. The sense of relief and elation that I was going to finish the sequences soon turned into panic.

The president asked, "What the hell is going on? Why did he stop answering questions?"

The response was silence. Everyone was just as much at a loss as the president.

Finally, Dr. Patel broke the silence and said in a panicked voice, "There is no reason for him to stop. For some reason he is just not answering the questions."

Back in the computer chamber, Hammerstein yelled at me through the door, "Enjoy the show, boy. I wanted you to see exactly how I treated your daddy." I watched in horror. I saw Hammerstein take out a tube with green liquid. Then I watched him pour the liquid onto a twelve-inch blade. Then I saw him plunge the blade into my daddy. I screamed at what I saw. I started to cry and put my hand over my mouth to cover my scream.

Hammerstein said, "I know you know what the poison is. You will be happy to know that his death will be painless, thanks to some modifications I made. But that is not the only modification I made. Instead of him dying in twenty-four hours, the normal time in which someone succumbs to such poison, your father's death will be much quicker. I also made sure that the normal antidote used for this type of poison will have no effect. His death today is certain. I know you know what the venom of a death adder does to a person's body. Your father will die today. And nothing you do in that chamber will prevent that."

The raw emotional sadness from what I saw and Hammerstein's words made me scream again. I then fell out of the chair onto my knees on the floor. Tears ran down my face like an uncontrollable river. I covered my face with my hands as I sobbed. I just couldn't continue what I was doing, answering the math problems. I was too hurt emotionally. This was what Hammerstein had intended. He knew that I had the intellect to answer the questions. But he also understood the power of emotion. He knew that seeing him give my father a slow, irreversible death would take an emotional toll on me, such a toll that I would not able to *focus*.

Now the computer began to readjust itself because I had stopped answering the complex math problems to activate the self-destruct. We were down to about four minutes before millions died. I knew this, but the loss of my greatest hero was too much for me to bear. I could not even lift myself off the floor.

Then another miracle happened. I took out a passport photo of my dad. The one he had given my brothers and me. At that moment somehow I did what my brothers and I had done earlier. I again remembered my father's teachings. I remembered the discussion we'd had about my abilities. I remembered again what he said when I told him how I wished I could have superstrength or superspeed like my brothers and how I was jealous of them. This time I remembered the conversation in more

230

detail. I remembered him smiling and coming down to one knee so we could be at eye level. He had me place my hand on my chest.

He said, "Son, what do you feel?"

I said, "MY heartbeat, Daddy."

Then he asked what I saw in the sky.

I said, "I see a bunch of birds flying in a pattern up north."

Then he pointed at a grove of trees and asked what I saw.

I said, "I see a bunch of trees, Daddy."

Then he pointed at a colony of ants on the ground.

I said, "Those are ants, Daddy."

Then he said something that was so obvious and yet so powerful. He said, "Everything we see, everything that is around us, everything that we see, feel, or hear— whether it's the trees, the birds, the flowers, your heartbeat, whether it's the waves of the ocean or the power of the sun—*is all mathematics. All of it.* You are a master of mathematics. As a master of mathematics, you can accomplish anything. In this world there are bad people who will do bad things. *You cannot let bad people do things that will distract you from doing the thing that you need to do when you need to do it.* You must be able to *focus* like a laser on what you need to do *when* you need to do it. Always remember *you are the universe, and the universe is you. You are mathematics, and mathematics is you.* You are jealous of your brothers? You got it wrong, son. It's your brothers who should be jealous of you."

That memory of my dad at that moment somehow gave me the strength to pull myself off the floor and get back in the chair. With tears coming down my face and clenched fists, I said with an intense, determined voice the phrase that my father had told me. Even with the madman continuing to taunt me in the background, I closed my eyes. I lifted my arms up to my sides and tilted my head back like I was making a prayer. Then I said out loud the words that Daddy had taught me to help me regain my focus. As I said the words, I remembered his voice saying them with me.

I said, "I...am...the universe. The universe is me. I...am...mathematics...and mathematics is...me." Now I knew what Jahvon felt like when he yelled, "This is my house." Saying those words gave me the push that I needed to overcome the emotional toll of seeing my father stabbed and poisoned. I was still hurting. But I was doing what my dad had taught me: focusing like a laser on the thing I needed to do when I needed to do it. What I needed to do was save the lives of millions, and I needed to do it *now*.

I had such focus at that moment that I began answering the questions correctly again and again. In fact, I was answering the questions with even more speed and accuracy than before.

From the sound of the computer, Hammerstein knew that the self-destruct mechanism was again being activated. He frantically tried to distract me. He yelled and taunted me. He cursed my father. He said many horrible things to me. None of it mattered because I was mathematics, and nothing was going to stop me from doing what I needed to do when I needed to do it. I wasn't going to let my daddy down.

Dr. Patel could see that I was again answering the questions. He yelled in excitement and joy, "He's doing it. He's doing it."

The energy field that had been created by the pylon's activation was fading. The energy from the four satellites was about to come through and down upon the earth. Only ninety seconds left. I began to answer the final set of math questions, solving the problems in less than three seconds each.

One by one each satellite in space received the self-destruct signal. One by one the satellites exploded. With each explosion, another solar blast disappeared from the pylon field. The president, his staff, Dr. Patel, and people all over the world pumped their fists in the air and cheered.

Hammerstein screamed in anger and frustration at the defeat of his plan.

I did it. I destroyed the four satellites. Millions of people were saved from being incinerated. Hammerstein's plan was defeated.

I fell back in the chair with a big, "Whew."

Then what had happened to my dad hit me again. The emotions returned. Now, I thought to myself, *I can mourn.*

However, Hammerstein was not yet done. By activating the satellites' self-destruct, I had also activated all the locks on the doors in the facility. Every door that had been closed and locked now electronically unlocked.

Now Hammerstein was able to enter the chamber. He kicked open the door and looked at me with pure hate in his eyes. He ran at me and swung with his left hand, striking me. The blow was so hard that I was knocked off the chair onto the floor. He grabbed my little ninety-pound body and threw me across the room.

He said, "You freak. Just like your damn father, you got in the way of my plans. And just like your father, you are going to suffer for what you have done."

The madman then slapped me in the face, knocking me from one end of the chamber to the other. Blood flowed from my nose and mouth. I wished at that moment I had Jahvon's strength to rip this evil monster apart. But I did not have Jahvon's strength or his near indestructibility. I could not take much more of this.

Hammerstein marched toward me slowly. He pulled his twelve-inch blade out of the sheath on his left hip.

No doubt it was the same blade he had used on my dad.

Hammerstein grabbed me by the throat with his right hand. His grip was like steel around my little skinny neck. He picked me up and slammed me against the wall. I could not breathe. My feet flailed in the air. I did not know whether he was going to stab me to death or strangle me. I was sure I was going to die.

He put the knife three inches from my eyeballs and said with pure hatred in his voice, "Look, boy, look. See the blood on my blade? That's the blood of your father. This is the same blade that I used to gut your father's comrades years ago. The same poisoned blade that I stabbed him with. I am going to add your blood to his on my blade." Then he looked at the picture of my father that I dropped on the floor when he first attacked me. He said, "That damn Navy SEAL grunt may have been your father. But you know how the old saying goes. I...brought you...into this world...and I will take...you...out." Then he raised his left hand with the blade high up in the air over his head. I knew I was going to die. I closed my eyes with tears coming down my cheeks. I cried because I did not want to die. But I was prepared. I felt a sense of peace of having helped save the lives of millions. I was ready. I waited for the blade to come down upon me.

Then, at that moment, another miracle happened. Both Hammerstein and I were surprised to hear a yelling

235

coming closer and closer. It was a loud scream: "Kiai!" Hammerstein did not recognize the voice. But I did.

Hammerstein turned to his right, toward the sound.

It was Joshua. He had come back for me.

Joshua had run at a high rate of speed to get back to the facility. He tracked me on the device I gave him and found the corridor that Hammerstein took. He ran at our evil creator, jumped in the air, and executed the same flying sidekick that he had always tried to mimic but never could—the one performed by Bruce Lee in the movie, *Chinese Connection*. This time he executed it perfectly. He rose four feet in the air and planted his right foot squarely on Hammerstein's face.

The force of the blow knocked Hammerstein over the banister, and he fell to a lower level in the computer chamber. His blade clattered to the ground.

Hammerstein's icy hand no longer crushed my throat. At last, gasping, I was able to breathe again.

After kicking Hammerstein, Joshua landed on his feet and then jumped into a fighting stance, ready if Hammerstein tried to charge up the steps.

The madman was momentarily stunned, but he seemed to recover pretty quickly. He looked as if he would rush back up the stairs to attack us. However, before he could do that, I walked to the foot of the steps. Once Hammerstein and I made eye contact, he paused. I'm not really sure what made him pause at that moment.

Perhaps it was the rage I felt toward him. The rage for what he had done to so many innocent people, especially my dad. I then said something to this evil madman. They were the last words he would ever hear.

I said, "You were so determined to kill me that you failed to notice that the fifth satellite is still operational. I not only ordered the self-destruct for the four main satellites, but I put in the commands for the self-destruct for the fifth satellite as well. But not before I made sure that the Dawn of the Shadow never again uses this facility to threaten the world."

Joshua said with fear in his voice, "*Huh?*"

At the same time I saw in Hammerstein's eyes something I had never seen there before: fear.

Hammerstein and Joshua were both troubled by what I had said. They both understood.

"I managed to hack into the fifth satellite. I programmed it to self-destruct but not before ordering it to target this facility and destroy it."

Hammerstein gasped in disbelief. Joshua gasped even louder.

I pointed at the holographic screen. It showed the fifth satellite moving into position over the facility.

Then I said, "As you can see, the fifth satellite has been moving into position ever since you came into this chamber to kill me. Had you been aware of your surroundings, you would have noticed. You might have had time to leave this facility alive." Then I said in a defiant and loud voice, "Always be aware of your surroundings. That's a lesson I learned from my daddy."

Hammerstein nervously looked at the screen on the ceiling. He saw the fifth satellite move above the facility.

Joshua picked me up, lifted me over his shoulder, and began to run out of the chamber as fast as he could.

Hammerstein, knowing what was about to happen and that he could not do anything to stop it, realized he was about to die. The fear and certainty of imminent death caused a predictable reaction from Hammerstein. He screamed.

As Joshua ran, carrying me, we heard Hammerstein scream.

The fifth satellite erupted down upon the facility, targeting the computer chamber. A powerful blast of irresistible destructive solar energy came down and cut through the facility like a hot knife through butter. The madman died screaming. The intensity of the heat from the solar energy instantly incinerated Hammerstein and destroyed the chamber. Immense fireballs exploded through the facility, incinerating everything in their path.

The flames were chasing Joshua. He had the burden of carrying me.

I yelled, "Drop me so you can get out of here!" I was prepared to die. I did not want my brother engulfed in flames because he was trying to save me.

But Joshua would not have any of it. His response was a firm, "Shut the hell up."

Joshua was already tired from all the running he had done earlier. Now he had ninety extra pounds on his back: me. He ran as fast as he could. The flames were close behind. He managed to make his way to the control room, where my father had been held. Thankfully, our father had already been evacuated.

Two SEALs were still on the roof of the facility. The fireballs had not yet made their way to that part of the roof of the facility. At least not yet. The SEALs saw Joshua and me run into the control chamber.

One of the SEALs yelled, "Up here!"

Joshua saw them. They SEALs had taken out pistols and shot cables that attached to another part of the facility. A small military plane was coming with a hook to lift them to safety. It was a very advanced and sophisticated way of leaving a location quickly. They must have started the procedure when the fifth satellite moved to target the facility. Dr. Patel's monitors would have shown him what was happening, and he must have given the military warning.

Joshua did not hesitate to take the SEALs up on their offer to get out of the facility. Then he did something I did not expect. He used the momentum of his superspeed to run up the wall, while still carrying me on his back. Luckily, he only had to travel about twelve feet up. As he neared the top of the roof, the SEALs grabbed Joshua's arm and helped him up. One SEAL grabbed me and then the other SEAL held on to Joshua. The military plane came swooping down with the hook. The plane scooped all of us up and with not a moment to spare. As we soared away the whole facility become engulfed in flames. Then the fifth satellite exploded in the air. Now all five satellites had been destroyed.

As the SEALs flew us to safety, Joshua yelled to me a very important question: "What about Jahvon? Did he make it out all right? Where is he?"

I gave a slight smile and yelled back, "Jahvon will be fine. He is near indestructible, remember?"

While Joshua and I were escaping the facility, Jahvon was still in the lower level with Ajax.

Jahvon had lifted the wounded Ajax up in the air and said, "I am taking you to jail, bad guy." Then both Jahvon and Ajax were surprised by the sound of loud explosions; it was the fifth satellite blasting the facility. Jahvon and Ajax looked behind them to see a raging fireball racing toward them, incinerating everything in its path. Still holding Ajax over his head, Jahvon was shocked and did not know what to do. Ajax was perfectly aware of what was happening, and that knowledge made him scream. The solar energy in the form of a fireball engulfed both Jahvon and Ajax. Ajax

240

did not have the benefit of being a superpowered prodigy. Nor did Ajax have the benefit of being protected by the energy field. He was just a man. An evil man, but a man nonetheless. Although the intense solar heat did not harm Jahvon because of his near invulnerability, it destroyed Ajax. While holding Ajax in the air, Jahvon saw him scream as he was incinerated in his hands. Watching in horror, Jahvon felt something toward Ajax that just a few moments earlier he would not have thought it possible to feel: pity. The heat was so intense that there was nothing left of Jahvon to hold on to. He looked at his hands where just moments ago he'd been holding one of the most wanted criminals in the world. Now he held nothing but ash.

Everything around Jahvon was an inferno. His clothes had been incinerated as well. It was as if he were standing naked in hell. Jahvon then decided to leave the area, praying that I had somehow gotten out. Not realizing that Joshua had rescued me.

As Joshua and I and the SEALs holding us were pulled into the rescue plane, the pilot circled back around to see if there were any more survivors.

"I don't see how anyone could have survived that inferno," the pilot said.

We all looked. We saw a familiar, naked twelve-year-old kid with a big afro. It was our brother, Jahvon.

Joshua laughed and yelled with joy, "Jahvon is alive. He may be indestructible, but his clothes aren't."

241

Joshua and I were both happy to see our brother, even if he was in the buff.

A military helicopter picked Jahvon up. They gave him a blanket to wrap around his waist and took him to the same military location where the plane took us. It was also the same location where the SEALs had taken our father.

Chapter 18

Saying Good-Bye

When we all arrived at the military location, Joshua and I embraced Jahvon. We were all happy to be alive and together again. Joshua and Jahvon each described their individual battles and challenges this day. It was a cathartic moment for my brothers. They felt good about what they had accomplished, but they also had faced evil and saw death. Then my brothers noticed that I was not as joyful as they were. Jahvon and Joshua knew me well enough to know when something was bothering me.

Jahvon asked, "What's wrong, Jason?"

Joshua said, "Yeah, Jason, what's the matter? We saved the day and beat the bad guys."

Jahvon then said, "And the SEALs kept their promise and got daddy out."

Joshua enthusiastically agreed.

I looked at them and said nothing at first. I did not know how to tell them about our father. I just said, "Um, uh, hey, let's go find Daddy."

The military location was at a local airfield, not far from where we had stolen the news helicopter. The location was filled primarily with other Navy SEALs. The SEALs were very kind to us. They took us inside a makeshift medical facility, where we found our father lying in a bed with a doctor sitting next to him.

Jahvon and Joshua were absolutely thrilled to see our father. They yelled with joy, "Daddy, Daddy!" They ran up to him and gave him a big hug. Of course, Joshua got to him before Jahvon and me.

The Navy SEALs and the doctor let my family have some privacy. They knew what I already knew. What my brothers did not know. That Daddy was going to die.

Jahvon and Joshua could not stop talking about the challenges they had overcome in helping save millions of lives. They could not stop telling Daddy how they remembered his lessons and put them in action. My brothers Joshua and Jahvon, bless them, were so excited to be with Daddy. They were so happy about helping to save the lives of millions that they did not notice how weak Daddy looked, with sweat coming down his face.

Then I walked up to my father and gave him a kiss on the forehead and held his hand. My brothers saw that I was not smiling and laughing with joy the way they were. They saw that I was not telling Daddy about what I'd done to help stop the plans of Hammerstein.

Jahvon looked at me asked, "Jason, what's wrong, man?"

My father said, "Hammerstein told you, didn't he?"

A tear came down my cheek. I sobbed and said, "Yes, Daddy. He told me."

Joshua, looking back and forth from me to Daddy, asked, "Told you what, Jason? Told you what?"

Jahvon, just as confused as Joshua, also asked, "Yeah, Jason. He told you what?"

I did not have the strength to answer. I just put my head down and cried. That was when my father answered for me.

"My dear sons, I am about to die," he said with a sad smile.

Joshua and Jahvon's reaction was predictable. "What? How? That can't be. The SEALs rescued you. The bad guys lost. We won. You can't leave us, Daddy. Please don't leave us, Daddy." Their smiles were gone. Their laughter was quickly replaced with sobs. They were confused and distraught. I had no words to comfort them. Then my father, even in his dying state, was able bring my brothers some sort of calm.

He grabbed my brothers' hands, placed a finger to each of their mouths, and said, "Shhh."

This enabled my brothers to somewhat calm down for the moment. Then my father smiled and said, "It's OK, boys. It's OK. It's...it's just my time. I have taken you as far as I can take you. I have been poisoned, and I am going to die. So you must listen to me. My dear Jahvon, Joshua, and Jason. My beautiful, wonderful boys. My beautiful and wonderful prodigies. I am so proud of each you. A man could not ask for better sons than the ones I have. My sons saved the lives of millions of people today. That is a great thing. You are going to have to be even stronger now. Always look out for one another. Always strive to make a positive impact on society and help those less fortunate than you. Remember that you will always carry me inside you."

Then Daddy looked at me and said, "Jason."

I immediately responded, "Yes, Daddy."

"I am making you the leader of this family. Help guide your brothers. Joshua and Jahvon, you two will respect Jason's leadership."

My brothers both nodded while crying and hesitantly said, "Yes...yes, Daddy."

Then my father said, "I want you to take the video recording I made to a man whose name and address I left in my trunk. You will know who the man is when he plays the video."

My father then paused and looked at each of us. It was clear that he was about leave us. His voice became even weaker. The poison was taking him from us. Daddy smiled and said, "You know...there was a time in my life when I thought there was no better way to die than to die fighting for my country. I was wrong. I know now that there is no better way to die than to die in the arms of one's children." Still smiling, he put his hands on each of our faces and gave us the last two commands that he would give us. The first was, "Big kiss for Daddy." We each gave him a kiss on the cheek as he gave each of us a kiss on ours. Then Daddy sat up in his bed with what little strength he had and opened his arms. He then gave his second and last command, a command that we had always enjoyed and carried out without hesitation. The command was, "Big hug for Daddy." The three of us came into him. Jahvon was on his right, I was in the middle, and Joshua was on his left. Daddy wrapped his arms around us, as he had every day for most of our lives. The four of our heads all came together as we embraced our father, not wanting to let go of him.

Then it happened. Daddy took one last deep breath, and my brothers and I felt the strength of his embrace slowly go limp. We gently lowered his head back down on the bed. His eyes were still open. I closed his eyelids. Jahvon and Joshua dropped their heads on Daddy's now lifeless chest, crying and screaming incoherently. I put my forehead on my father's forehead while tears flowed out of my eyes, and I made a promise.

"Don't worry, Daddy...I will lead them. We will make you proud. We will always be your prodigies for *good*."

In a few short moments, my brothers had gone from being on top of the world to feeling worse than they had ever felt in their lives. Our anchor, our foundation, our greatest hero was now dead.

I don't remember how long my brothers and I stayed holding our father's body, crying our hearts out. Even the battle-hardened and tough Navy SEALs were a little choked up at my father's passing. They did not know my father, but he was one of theirs. Like them, he was a Navy SEAL.

The SEAL commander approached us. While the other SEALs gathered around, the commander dropped down to one knee.

He said, "I am sorry for your loss, boys. I truly am."

Chapter 19

Daddy's Final Instructions

Days later, we were brought in front of the president of the United States and his national security team. We were treated well. Our father was buried at Arlington National Cemetery. He was given full military honors for his service to the country. My brothers and I were given really nice suits to wear at his funeral. The honor guard of the military folded the American flag in a small triangle in honor of our father. The uniformed soldier came to where my brothers and I were sitting, in the front, facing our father's casket. I was between my brothers. President Jamison, General Madson, and the SEALs who had got my father out of the facility were all present. One of the uniformed soldiers handed the folded American flag to President Jamison. The president then walked up to where my brothers and I were sitting and bent on one knee. He held out the flag to me, and my brothers and I all put our hands on the flag.

Then the president warmly said, "On behalf of a grateful nation, we offer you our deepest condolences on the loss of your father."

My brothers and I, with tears still in our eyes, simultaneously said, "Thank you."

The president then let go of the flag, and I kept it in my arms. My brothers and I felt sad, but we appreciated the honors that my father received. No one would ever truly understand how much he had done for this nation and the world. If not for him, my brothers and I would have grown up under the tutelage of a madman; we would have become hardcore killers, creating terror in the world. Instead, thanks to our father, we were committed to help make the world a better place.

After the ceremony, my brothers and I were invited into the White House. President Jamison along with General Madson wanted to talk to us about the future. As the president and the general spoke, their intentions became clear were. They wanted my brothers and me to be weapons working on behalf of the government.

They sent us to a house in Virginia. It was a nice, big house. There we would live and begin a form of retraining for the needs of the US government. We were under constant watch. There were Secret Service guards all around. I also knew that drones were watching the house.

A few days later, the president, while conducting a staff meeting that included General Madson, got a disturbing message. All the Secret Service agents and other government staff assigned to watch my brothers and me had been found unconscious. My brothers and I were gone.

We had left behind a package for the president and the general. The package contained a video recording. It also contained a phone.

When the president played the video, they found a recording of me politely saying the following: "Mr. President, General Madson, we are not going to become weapons for you to use. We are going to live our lives in a way that we see fit and on our own terms. We will help you fight evil when we can. Even though Nicholas Hammerstein and Ajax are dead, we all know the Dawn of the Shadow is still out there. We also know that my father's SEAL team was set up twelve years ago in Syria and that the traitor was never discovered. I suspect that whoever the Dawn of the Shadow had in the government then is still in the government today. So, you can see why we won't work directly with you. Make no mistake, though, we will fight the Dawn of the Shadow and other evil in the world, but on our terms. Now I know that you will try to find my brothers and me. That is why I took some precautions. First I took the liberty of hacking into the entire computer network throughout the government, including the CIA and the Pentagon. I erased everything they had on us."

The president and the general both yelled, "What?"

"I also built special equipment for me and my brothers that will prevent us from ever showing up anywhere on any camera. If you ever need to communicate with us, I left you this cell phone that I personally made. With it you will be able to call me. But you won't be able to

251

track me, thanks to the special features that I built into the phone, which are just too complicated for me to explain now. Just please keep in mind, gentlemen, *we...are...on...the...same...side.* But, like I said, my brothers and I have to live our lives on our terms and not yours. We will keep in touch. As you look for us, know we will also be watching you."

At that moment, Jahvon stepped in front of the camera and, with two fingers, pointed to his eyes and then at the camera, a gesture directed at the president and the general.

I finished by saying, "Thank you again for honoring our father. Good-bye." The recording stopped. Then, thanks to some modifications I'd made to the disk, the recording self-destructed.

The president ordered his team to find us. Even though he knew they would not.

A week after my brothers and I escaped the "living arrangements" of the federal government, we carried out the last instruction that our father left us.

We went to the home of the man whose address Daddy had left with the video recording he'd made before he died.

The home was huge and beautiful, in a nice area with lots of vegetation. Whoever lived in the house was clearly a person of wealth. The home was in Scarsdale, New York. The man we were looking for was named

Kevin Bullock. We still had not watched the video, so we did not know the significance of this man to our father. We would soon find out.

When we got to the door, we rang the bell. We could hear a man yelling in the background, "All right, all right, I'm coming, dammit." The door was opened by a white man with brown hair and a goatee. He looked to be of average build and was in a wheelchair. His legs were gone from the knees down.

He looked at us with a surprised look and said, "Can I help you?"

I politely apologized for the intrusion and told him that we had a message to deliver for a Mr. Kevin Bullock.

He said, "I'm Kevin Bullock." His first thought was that we were some runaway kids who were looking for shelter at his home. He thought that the story of a message for him was some hoax until I mentioned the name Jordan Reyes. The name of our father. When I mentioned the name, he looked like he saw a ghost. Then, after pausing for a few moments, he invited us in. As we walked into his home, my brothers and I noticed a lot of pictures of the man in military uniform. It was clear that he was a veteran. It was starting to make sense why our father would send us to him.

He told me to let him see the message. I took out the video disk. He put it into his DVD player in his living room. The living room was huge. He had a beautiful fifty-inch television. We all sat on the couch in the living room to watch the video. The video played, and my father appeared on the screen. We all took a deep breath. Seeing our father was emotional for my brothers and me. What surprising us was that Kevin Bullock seemed emotional as well.

When Kevin Bullock saw the image of my father, he gasped and said, "My God...Jordan?" It was clear that this man knew our father.

My brothers and I watched in amazement. As the video played, it was as if my father were communicating from beyond the grave. We listened intently to my father's words to Mr. Bullock:

"Hello, Kevin, I know you have a lot of questions. I know you are wondering why I never contacted you. Well, it's a long story. One that I don't have time to give you full details on. Just know that the three boys in front of you are my greatest treasure. They...are my sons. Know also that at the time that you are seeing this video...I—" Our dad hesitated. "It means that I would already be dead. I did not die in a helicopter crash in Syria. None of my unit did. We were captured and tortured by the Dawn of the Shadow. Eventually, they killed my entire team. Somehow I escaped. I escaped with my children. I did not contact you because my boys and I were being hunted by the Dawn of the Shadow. I could not and would not at the time risk your life. You are the best friend I ever had. You are more than that. You are my brother. You once told me that you owed me for all the times I saved your life. Well now, my brother, I'm looking to collect on your promise. My boys have very special abilities that you will soon become aware of. But despite their incredible abilities, they are still...they are still just kids. They need some type of father figure in their lives who can continue to guide them through this crazy thing we call life. They still need some normalcy and stability in their lives. Please give them that. Take them to a basketball game. Take them fishing. Teach them about girls. Be that shoulder that they can lean on when they are down. Most of all, just give them a home. Because of who my sons are and what they can do, I am sure they will still be hunted even after I am gone. If you take my boys in, you must understand that your life could be in danger." My father became emotional. "But Kevin, I have no one else that I can trust. They have the potential to make this world a better place. That potential must be protected and nurtured. I am trusting you with them. I am trusting you with my greatest treasure, my sons. My little prodigies."

Then in the video at that moment, we all saw Joshua and Jahvon coming into our father's bedroom. Joshua and Jahvon gave him a hug and kiss and told him good night. Then I came in to do the same.

I marveled as I watched myself ask my father the question I had asked him that night: "Daddy, who are you talking to?"

The response we all saw on the video was the response I remembered. "An old friend."

I gave my father a hug and a kiss and I left him alone.

Then I saw on the video—just as I had when I looked through the cracked door that day—my father raise his inverted fist, as if giving a fist bump to a friend. Now we all knew who that friend was. My father concluded the video by saying, "Good-bye, Kevin."

As the video ended, Kevin gasped. He remembered his past with my father. He remembered how he and my father had joined the military at the same time. He remembered how they went through basic training together. How they went through training to become Navy SEALs together. He remembered how my father would always get the better of him when they sparred. He remembered how my father had a hard time getting a helmet to fit his head and how Kevin would joke about my daddy having a big head. He remembered how they saw combat together in Iraq and Africa when they went on missions together as Navy SEALs. He remembered how my father was always the better soldier and how my father saved his life on a number of occasions. He remembered the last mission they had together, when he lost his legs in an explosion. He remembered how my father disobeyed orders to go back for him and how my father picked him up even though he had just had both legs blown off. He remembered how my father took him to safety and how my father yelled at him in that terrible moment about how he would not let him die. Kevin remembered when my father came to visit him at a military hospital, how he made it clear that he owed my father for all the times he had saved his life. He also remembered how he heard the news of my father's SEAL team being killed over twelve years ago in Syria. And how he had lost hope of ever hearing from his best friend again.

My brothers and I sat in silence. We did not know what would happen next. We did not know what memories Kevin had of our father or what Kevin was thinking at that moment. We thought that this Kevin Bullock was just some grumpy-looking man who might have known our father in the past but had no interest in taking in three strange boys. Then something happened that Joshua, Jahvon, and I did not expect.

Kevin Bullock, still facing the direction of the huge television that had just finished playing our father's message, lifted his right hand. It was an inverted fist. It was as if he were giving my father a fist bump.

After he lifted his fist, Kevin said in an emotional whisper, "You got it, brother."

Then he put his arm down and looked at my brothers and me individually. We kept quiet, still not sure what he would say or do. Finally, Kevin pointed at me and in a very gruff voice asked, "What is your name, kid?"

"Jason," I responded softly.

Then he said, "You got your daddy's eyes."

He turned to Joshua and pointed and asked in a commanding tone, "Hey, you, what's your name?"

Joshua hesitantly said, "Uh, Joshua."

Kevin responded by saying, "You got your dad's mouth and nose."

Then he looked at Jahvon and said, "And you, big guy, what is your name?"

Jahvon responded with an automatic "Jahvon."

Kevin looked at Jahvon closely and smiled and said, "Your name is Jahvon, huh? Well, Jahvon, you got your daddy's *big head*."

When Kevin said that, it made my brothers and me laugh. We needed that. It helped to break the ice between him and us. Kevin told us that he accepted our father's request. He told us about his friendship with our father. He told us about the history he shared with our father and how that history ran through his mind as he was watching our father's video. We told him who we were and what we could do. Kevin welcomed us into his home.

Our moving in with Kevin was the start of a new chapter in our lives. If our father trusted Kevin, then we were going to trust him as well. That's what we did. While Kevin was willing to look out for us, we were also going to look out for him.

Kevin was a very wealthy man. He came from a very wealthy family. Kevin always believed in public service. He had joined the military and received an honorable discharge for his injuries in combat. He now spent most of his time engaged in philanthropy. Kevin was willing to risk his life by taking us in. After what had happened to Mr. Ferrante, we understood why our father did not want to reach out to Kevin. Our father did not want to risk Kevin's life. However, Kevin was more than willing to risk his life for the children of his best friend.

Thanks to our father, we found a new home and ally. It seemed even in death our father was taking care of us. We knew that the future would have challenges for us. We knew that the government was looking for us. We knew that it would only be a matter of time before we would again confront the Dawn of the Shadow. However, we were not worried. My brothers and I were committed to continue living the vision instilled in us: to be prodigies of good and help make the world a better place. A vision that came from our father. Our greatest hero.

AUTHOR ALEX R. CASTRO

Alex Castro is a former New York City police officer and Wall Street stockbroker. Alex has dedicated his life to public service and firmly believes that in every child there is an inner prodigy for good. Currently, Alex R. Castro is a practicing attorney in New York City.